Hill of Slemish

ULIDIA

Hill of Dichu

Valley of
Sescnen
ain of Meath
Tara
Hill of Slane

Flame over Tara

Madeleine Polland

Flame over Tara

ILLUSTRATED BY
Omar Davis

SONLIGHT

The way you wish you'd been taught.

First Sonlight Curriculum edition published March 2004
by arrangement with the author. Reprinted April 2010.

Library of Congress Catalog Card Number 64-11285

ISBN 1-887840-55-9

For a catalog of Sonlight Curriculum materials for the
home school, write:

Sonlight Curriculum, Ltd.
8042 South Grant Way
Littleton, CO 80122-2705
USA

Or e-mail: catalog@sonlight.com

For my cousin, Father Joe,
who in the interests of this book
actually walked on the Hill of Tara.

Adze head will come,
Over the mad crested sea
His cloak hole headed
His staff crooked headed,
His table in the east of his house;
He will chant impiety from his table
And all his household will respond:
Amen, Amen.

Chapter One

For Macha, it was a day of happiness. Since she had been
a small child of four, she had lived as foster child according
to the Irish custom in the Household of her father's kinsman
Sescnen and his wife, Finola, sharing through the long
years the days and pastimes of her two foster sisters and
their brother, Benet. Today, on this bright day in the spring
season of the year four hundred and thirty-two, her foster
father had called her to him in the cool, early shadows of

his Hall, where the damp smoke of the fresh-kindled fire still crept about the rafters, and the sun had not yet struck in through the open door.

He saw her surprised expression as she looked about the almost empty Hall, the curtains still drawn across the sleeping rooms along the walls, and her foster father alone, without the company that should attend him always in his Hall, according to his position as Chieftain of a tribe.

"Yes, my daughter," he said, as he bent to take the kisses of her salutation on his cheek. "We are alone, and I have wished it so, because I have very important news for you this morning, and I wanted you to hear it from me in quietness."

She looked at him, watchfully.

"Yes, my father?"

Under the smooth curled locks of his graying hair, his gentle face was mild and sad. He was a man considerably older than her father, known through all the eastern land for his quietness and wisdom.

"So many years," he said to her, and smiled, warm with affection. "So many years we have had you, since your feet were small for stumbling up the long slopes of the dun, and you were weightless on my back if I should carry you. But now, Macha, our daughter, you are near to fourteen years, and it is time for us to part with you. To send you back to your father's house, so that he and your mother may think of your marriage, and prepare you for it. You are to go home."

"To go home?" The girl stared at him, and fear and delight struggled together across her soft, freckled face. In the first confused rush of her feelings she looked about her, and was glad of the kindness that had led him to tell her alone. "To go home," she said then again. "To Tara," she added then, on a soft breath of wonder and disbelief.

In the long years in the household of Sescnen, she had

been truly happy, taking for granted the custom of her fosterage, but she knew that she was the daughter of Labran of the Long Memory, Chief Judge to Leary, the High King of Erin, and under all her happiness was the knowledge that one day she would go back to her father's house on the green slopes of the sacred Hill of Tara below the dwelling of the King.

For a long moment she said nothing, all her mixed feelings surging in her mind.

"Are you not pleased?" Sescnen asked her then, looking at her with gentle concern and lifting his voice a little against the clatter of the bondwomen who tended the smoking fire. Since the message had come to him in the dawn, bidding the girl to be returned to her parents, he had been thinking of her; wondering how she would face the change. He knew she was devoted to his family and his wife, Finola, and he had feared for grief and dismay.

To his relief, the face she turned up to him was nothing more than a little fearful and touched with excitement.

"Sescnen, my father," she said, and her voice was breathless, a small voice at all times, and light. "I am sad to leave you after all these long years when my growing feet have walked your house." She had got the formal words out and now she rushed on. "But you and the family will visit with us in Tara, as my parents have come here. So we are not parted forever." He was not sure if she spoke to comfort herself or him, but her slight smile widened and her eyes glowed at him. "I am longing to see the sacred Hill, and the dwellings of the High King, and all the great places of Tara. But marriage—" The bright eyes grew shadowed and the smile faded and the freckled face was apprehensive. Sescnen laid a hand on her head.

"It will not be at once, little one. All things come gently and in time. You will be ready for it."

Life was rising in the Hall behind them, people stirring

9

in the sleeping rooms along the walls, and women laying dishes on the small tables for the morning meal. Against the clatter, Macha stood in silence and watched, knowing in that moment that she would really be leaving him; and the family and all the unthinking years of her happy childhood in this small dun above the cold, tumbling sea.

"Oh, my father," she said then, and her voice was thin, and she laid her head down on his breast in the honored gesture of long love and respect. A moment he stroked the soft, red hair.

"It will be well, my daughter," he said gently. "It will be well. Now I see that the meal is almost ready. The pots are on the table and the men are coming in. People gather about us. Go now to the grianin and find your foster mother, and tell her and the children your news."

Blinking the sudden tears from her lashes, she turned obediently and left him, pausing in a moment to look back.

"How long until I go?" she asked him.

"Your father will come for you in about fourteen days from now, when the great Spring Festival is past at Tara."

She nodded and went on out, into the fresh sun where the sweet reek of turf rose from all the new-lit fires around the dun, and the thin threads of smoke above them flickered in the small wind from the sea. At first she walked abstracted, her head down, returning absently the morning greetings of the people of the dun. Then gradually a slow smile began to creep across her face and the light brown eyes kindled into pleasure.

Tara! Her foster family were very dear to her, but even though Sescnen was kinsman to her father and also to the High King himself, he was only the Chieftain of a small tribe, and his dun was neither large nor wealthy. But Tara! That would be quite different, and indeed the more she thought of it, what was wrong with the idea of marriage and a household of her own on the green fields below the palace. Who would her father choose for her? There were so many whom it might be, among the young nobles who lived on Tara. A warrior would be nice! She gave a little skip of pure excitement and her long hair danced against her back, and by the time she reached the grianin, or ladies' bower, her freckled face had lost its sadness and was bright with pleasure in the future.

She found it difficult to concentrate through the long morning of study and the afternoon of needlework, but in the end it was over and she was free to walk with Benet along the edges of the sea, dodging the tumbling waves of the high tide that foamed along the pale stretches of the sandy beach and surged up the mouth of the small river below the lowest walls of the dun. As there was peace this spring day, and no hint of threat, the big gates in the lower palisade stood open and the people came and went between the dun and the fishing village at the mouth of the river.

Macha stood in the edges of the waves and snatched at her sandal strings, wanting to match her mood of excitement with the cold agony of the water rushing round her ankles and the unstable sand sliding away between her toes.

"Benet!" she shouted as she flung her shoes away. "Benet, are you sorry I'm to go away?"

Benet was at this time a boy of eleven, with the same mild, quiet face as his father. In the dun, they called him "the gentle one," for although he fought and tumbled with all the other boys, and took full part in their warriors games, he was never known to lose his temper, facing all his young life with an amiable smile and some strange unchildlike steadfastness of character.

He stood sunk up to his ankles in the soft, white sand, with the wind trailing his brown hair across his face, and looked in silence at Macha, dancing in the foam.

"Are you sorry I'm going, Benet?" she called again, lifting

her voice against the wind and the crying of the gulls along the endless shore.

He smiled at her then and for a moment it was as if he were the older; standing there so quietly with kindness in his eyes for the tousled girl capering in the sea, with her hair tattered by the wind, and her skirts of saffron linen gathered damp and crumpled in her hands.

"Wouldn't I be sorry," he said then, "if they said the sun wouldn't rise for me again after tomorrow, or some certain day? Wouldn't I weep at the thought of the darkness?"

She stopped in her leaping over the waves, and stood with the wet, icy sand crumbling underneath her feet, arrested by the strange formality of his words. Looking at him, she saw through her own excitement the clear sadness in his young face. Pity struck her and she forgot her new importance, and her hands grew limp on her yellow skirts, trailing wet and dark in the water as she rushed out to him.

"Oh, Benet! Don't grieve for me like that! I will not be very far away. Even when I have a husband, you can visit with me in my own household, and see the Rath of the Kings, and Micorta, the great Banquet Hall, and all the splendors of the Royal Dun. You would enjoy that?"

Desperately she peered close into his face, almost as if she had not seen him before, suddenly conscious of the unhappiness of his dark blue eyes under their black lashes.

His sadness caught her, too, and she did not know how she would ever bring herself to leave any of them. Tears rose hot and thick to choke her throat and spike the edges of her lashes.

Benet moved back a little to sit down in the cool, shifting sand above the sea.

"Now I've made you unhappy, Macha," he said remorsefully as she followed and flopped down beside him, scrubbing the tears from her eyes with the edge of her cloak, her pale cheeks reddening with the rubbed salt of the spray. "I think I'm only jealous of you," he added.

"Jealous?" Amazement widened her tawny eyes. "Why? Do you want to get married yourself? Men are not married as young as you! How could you keep a wife, without land or cattle?"

She looked at him as if she thought he had left his senses with the touch of a Druid wisp, and Benet laughed out loud, clear and light in the wide air, flinging himself back in the soft sand.

He laughed again and shook his head, and his white, uneven teeth closed on his lower lip. "Oh no, Macha! I don't want to get married! Who would have me?" His face grew serious then, and Macha watched him, his eyes sad and distant as he stared out over the crested water. "No, I'm jealous because you know what you are going to do. You know what your life is for, and the rules are there for you to live it by." Now the girl was utterly bewildered, staring at this Benet, who talked all of a sudden like an old man, the grave words odd and impossible from his round, childish face. "You will get married," he went on. "It is all laid down. You will marry some good man of your father's choosing, and settle down in a dwelling at Tara and raise your family round you. It is all there. You have nothing to doubt or think about."

Macha was truculent, bewildered and upset by this strange, unchildlike boy whom she had never seen before.

"Well, and what is wrong with that?" she demanded of him fiercely, eyeing him as though amazed that he could look the same as ever and yet talk such nonsense.

"Nothing, nothing. Don't be angry with me. I only said I think you lucky. When I try to look into *my* future, I see nothing at all."

The girl still stared at him, her wet skirts in her hand. What had got into him? She was impatient.

13

"You have a future just as clear as mine! You are your father's son, and will live to take his place and rule the tribe as he does now! You don't need me to tell you this," she added more gently.

She wanted to reassure him, to see this old-looking, unhappy face clear, so that she herself could be happy again, as she had been before he spoke. But Benet rolled over on his face, grabbing at the soft sand and watching it pour out through his fingers.

"I don't know that I want that! I know nothing! I look into my future and it is like a thick cloud, like a Druid augury by fire and smoke, but for me the smoke clears to no picture. I see no picture, no future."

Macha shivered suddenly in the bright day, touched unwillingly by his discontent. With no idea what to say or how to deal with him, she stood up and made a great fuss of brushing the fine sand from her clothes and wringing the water from the ends of her skirts, glancing out over the sea in desperate hope of something she could find to talk to him about. At once she straightened and forgot her clothes, staring out over the water.

"Benet! A boat! A big one, and a strange one! Coming for the river mouth!"

Benet leapt to his feet. He was a boy again, his fears of the future forgotten, his face as old only as his eleven years.

"Where?"

"There!" Macha pointed. "They are just lowering the sail."

"Ah—I see her! They are getting out the sweeps to manage the tide at the mouth of the river. It is someone who knows his way in! But the boat is strange!"

They stood puzzled, watching the vessel as she made her way toward the small estuary of the river on the far side of the dun, coming easily on the green, white-crested springtime sea, her long oars dipping to the rising tide.

"Macha, look at all the people in it!" Benet drew closer to her. "What can it be? No trading vessel would have all those aboard her!"

"And they are all in white," Macha answered in a while, as puzzled as he. "All in white clothes. Are they all Druids?"

"There is one who stands in the prow alone, and he has something which glitters round his brow."

Even as he spoke, the declining sun struck a blaze of brilliance from the head of the small, solitary figure in the prow of the distant boat. Macha looked for her shoes.

"Come, brother," she said, "we'll see what this is all about. It will reach the beaching just as we do, if we run." The boy was off before her, ignoring the cries of his young sisters from the sand dunes, and side by side he and Macha raced excitedly off along the sands toward the river, and the spot where the strange vessel could be expected to make landfall.

Already, by the time they had skirted the lower walls of the dun, and the huts of the fisher people below it, and come to the river mouth, there was a crowd of people gathered. In murmuring curiosity, they watched the boat that was now coming close inshore, her sweeps withdrawn and her helmsman watching to beach her on the soft white sand below the harbor huts.

Macha cut across toward them over the drying grounds, brushing aside the hanging nets, half noticing the smell of tar and fish sharp on the cooling wind, and realizing suddenly that Benet had come to a stop and she had left him far behind.

"Come closer, Benet! Come closer!" She dodged backward and forward, her eyes darting between Benet and the boat, urging him nearer. "What strange people they are! We have never seen such before! Come nearer!"

In spite of all her urging, Benet stayed where he had stopped, apart from the curious crowd, silent and still on a small rise of the dunes, with his blue eyes wide on the men who now leapt out into the foaming shallows from the high-sided, foreign-looking craft.

The rough, long-bearded men of the village crowded close and stared at the strangers in amazement and suspicion. They muttered and wondered and drew back, and then crowded close again in their irresistible curiosity. The men from the sea all wore white robes, strange, loose garments that hung full above their trews, now darkened with the sea water as the first of them waded up on to the sand. They were smiling and friendly, speaking amiably in their own language to the crowd of astonished people on the shore.

On the small sandhill, the boy Benet stood alone, bright and solitary in his blue tunic, his brown curls lifting to the wind and his wide, incredulous eyes resting only on the man who stood alone in the prow of the vessel. This man wore white like all the others, a one-piece garment that looked as though his cloak were taken and a hole cut for his head. About his brow rested a band of gold from which rose a flat blade like the head of an ax, splintering and glittering in the last light from the sun above the western hill. In his hand he held a tall crook-headed staff, bright with the same sunlit gold, and at him and him alone did Benet look, watching steadily as one of the bigger men in the boat came to him and lifted him, carrying him dry-shod through the shallow water to the shore, and setting him down before the crowd; not a very tall man, but strong and agile-looking, with a brown, weatherbeaten face. The boy wondered why he could not have climbed out like all the others, and waded ashore from the beached boat.

Macha rushed back to him and seized him by the arm, her pale face pink with excitement.

"What is he, that he cannot step into the sea like other men? Who are they?" She could neither watch nor talk enough. "Look, Benet! Oh look! He is going to speak to us, the small one with the adze head on his brow! Is he the leader? Oh come *on*, Benet! What is wrong with you?"

When she pulled at his arm and he still refused to come, she gave him her attention for a moment, looking at his wide eyes and his rapt, astonished look.

"What is it? If they are strange, then come and see them. They are peaceful, they have no weapons. There's nothing to fear, Benet!"

"I am not afraid." His voice was almost absent. "Adze head," he said then. "Oh, Macha, that is it! We are seeing a prophecy fulfilled; we are living the words of the Druids."

"You talk no sense!"

She was impatient, irritable at missing the excitement of hearing the man speak, but there was something strange in Benet's face that told her to have patience, and when he seized her in turn and began to race her toward the open gates of the dun, she came with him with only one last backward glance.

"We must get my father," he cried as he ran. "He will know of it. It was he who told me!"

The long, green eastern slopes of the hill were now in shadow, but the sun still struck golden from the west, lighting the bush-crowned tops of all the raths inside the dun, and on every earthen wall in the late, warm glow, the people were gathered, watching the distant scene below them on the shore.

"Who are they, and whence do they come?"

From their high walls the people leaned over and shouted to the running children, and Macha, full of her news, would have stopped to chatter. But the boy would have none of them, shaking his head and pounding on up the long, darkening slopes until he reached his father's own rath at the very top. Here Sescnen stood like all his people, on the watchman's rampart of the wall, his wife and children at his side, staring with the others through the gathering dusk.

Benet was too breathless for the last climb up the wooden ladder. He stood at the bottom and held to the rough timber of the rails and gasped for his breath.

"My father!" he managed to shout at last, and only then did Macha come panting up beside him. His soft, sunflushed face was white, and his hair curled tight round his hot, damp forehead. Sescnen came, and looked down on him in silence and waited for him to speak.

"My father," he shouted, and it was as though in the clear, green evening, the whole dun fell silent with his father to hear what he had to say. Only a solitary blackbird piped of spring from the elms beyond the Hall. "My father, have you seen them?"

"I have seen them."

Father and son looked at each other, and the girl looked from one to the other with some sense that what they said was of desperate importance; some unhappy and yet excited certainty that from this urgent moment on the rath of Sescnen, nothing would ever be the same again.

"Tell me again, father," cried Benet, and his young voice rang like a bell in the clear silence. "What was it the Druids said? I have forgotten! Tell me the prophecy!"

He pushed back the sweat-damp hair from his forehead and watched his father, who turned from him a moment and looked down at the shadowy figures by the sea, and then turned back. His face had the same stunned look of settled amazement as his son's. Slowly and clearly Sescnen spoke, and from all the higher raths in the dun, astonished faces lifted themselves, ghostly white, to listen.

Adze head will come,
Over the mad crested sea
His cloak hole headed
His staff crooked headed,

His table in the east of his house;
He will chant impiety from his table
And all his household will respond:
Amen, Amen.

There was a long silence when he stopped, with no sound but the wind in the trees along the crest of the hill and the far murmur of the sea, and the higher, urgent murmur of the crowd below them on the beach. Through it, father and son still looked at each other.

"Go down, my son," said Sescnen at last. His voice was quiet now, carrying through the stillness. "Go down and bid him welcome in my name. Bid them all welcome, and bring them all up to my house."

Chapter Two

The now silent people moved apart to let them go, and on
Benet's bidding the strangers came across the shore and
into the dun, their white robes gleaming in the failing light.
Although many of the wild, bearded faces of the villagers
were hostile and suspicious, no hand was raised against
them since they walked with the son of the Chief. Their
leader smiled about him as he walked, leaning on his long
staff and raising his right hand in some gesture that was

strange to the watching crowd. Before him Benet moved with bright, dazed eyes, as though he was just risen from a long sleep.

Sescnen waited for them in the shadows of his Hall, the evening light forgotten in the curiosity that was bright on all the faces of his household gathered with him. Firelight flickered on the sea-stained robes of the strangers and blazed scarlet in the golden adze above the leader's brow, leaving his strong, handsome face in shadow. Benet left him, and went to stand in his place beside his father on the other side of the fire. The man smiled at him and thanked him for his safe conduct, and Macha, listening to his Irish, found it fluent and easy to understand, but overlaid with some turn of tongue which she had never heard before.

"You are welcome in my house," Sescnen said to him, "and the women are preparing food. You have traveled long, and your clothes are stained by the sea. Will you and your companions bathe before you eat? The bath house is ready."

His mild eyes roamed over them all, as wide with curiosity as any of his peoples', but he was the Chieftain of the dun, and having made the strangers welcome in his homestead, courtesy forbade that he should ask them questions as to who they were, or whence they came. He mustered his patience as best he could, and resigned himself to wait until they were rested and eaten and perhaps prepared to talk.

But the leader with the golden adze looked at him across the fire, and leaned as he spoke on the long crook-headed staff of the prophecy.

"First of all I will tell you who we are, and let the word go out among your people, that all may know that I have come."

He was not a tall man, as Macha had noticed when he left the boat, but he gave a sense of height by some grace and strength of bearing, and a clear, commanding quality about his voice that carried into every corner of the crowded Hall. In the smoky shadows, she craned to see his face, getting a sense only of a mild countenance like Sescnen's own, above the forked beard of reddish brown.

"It is not necessary as my guest, that you should tell me anything."

"I would prefer it so, for I am here to have all Erin know of me, and of Him in whose Name I come. I am Magnus Sucatus Patricius, Citizen of Rome. In your tongue, my name is Patrick, consecrated Bishop of the Church of Christ, and I am come to bring the Word of God to the people of this land, and give them knowledge and understanding and the teaching of truth."

Sescnen, not understanding, raised his hands in a small gesture and groped for the courteous word.

"You speak our language well, stranger."

Patrick turned and faced into the crowded shadows, where a blur of faces watched him in silence.

"I have been among you before for many years. A Roman Citizen I was born, in Britain, on the shores of the Western Sea. While I was still a boy, a youth barely able to speak, I was taken captive by the Irish and brought into slavery." His clear, melodious voice lifted to the smoke-black rafters, and the fascinated people crept a little closer. "Many years I tended sheep for my master on the slopes of the northern hills, and there in my long solitary days, I prayed."

They did not understand him, but the compelling voice held them, and no one spoke to question.

"And there one night," he went on, "as I slept among my sheep, I heard a voice speak to me. 'It is well that you fast,' it said, 'for soon you will go to your own country.' And again later, it said to me, 'See, your ship is ready.' And I escaped and went to my own people, but I could not stay with them. I will tell you why."

He looked all around the watching faces in the Hall, formless in the gathering dark, and the warm smile of his affection embraced every one of them, even to those who, a little fearful, stood beyond the open doors, and would not come inside. He held out his hands as though he gathered them all into one.

"You called me," he said, simply, and every single listening man felt that he spoke to him alone. "You called me." There was no sound in the packed Hall save the sighing crumble of a falling log, and beyond the open doors the tumbling murmur of the high spring sea. "In my sleep, I heard again the voices of the Irish speaking to me, in the voices of those I had known when I tended my sheep near the wood of Voclut beside the Western Sea. And they cried with one mouth, 'We ask thee, boy, come and walk with us once more.'"

The firelight was red and steady in the disc above his brow and his eyes roamed over them all, holding them. They waited breathless for his next word, caring nothing that they did not understand him.

"Thanks be to God," he said into the silence. "After many years, the Lord gave them according to their cry!"

Macha saw his face in the clear light as he stood for a moment in silence, letting his words fall into their minds. He looked very tired, his hair draggled from the sea under the glittering band, and salt crusted round the edges of his lips. She gazed at him as he looked over them all, the very first of his mission, and suddenly, with an abruptness that was terrifying, she felt the importance of her home and Tara and her husband sliding away. Nothing in this instant seemed to matter except to stay within sight of this quiet steadfast face and within the sound of the beautiful voice, watching and listening in patience until she should understand the things he spoke of.

She looked around her, shaken and overwhelmed by her

sudden feelings, wondering if her foster mother or anybody else might look at her and see a change, even in her face. But every eye was fixed on the man beside the fire, and she turned back to him. He passed a hand across his forehead as if weariness took him at last, and then reached aside for a stool at the corner of the square hearth, and Sescnen reproached himself for his lack of manners, that he had not bidden him sit.

Patrick smiled at him then, a strange, almost shy smile in so resolute a face, and as the full darkness of the spring night took the Hall, he began to tell them of the God who had called him to them; of His truth and His life and death, which had all been for His people. His persuasive voice was hoarse with weariness, but it filled every darkest corner and reached its spell even to the women who cooked in the kitchen building, so that they left their pots and moved in to hear him, and the cool night had filled the Hall and the high-piled fire crumbled to pink ash before he stopped. Yet none had stirred to kindle the lights or break the silence. At a gesture from Finola a woman moved at last and lit the four tall candles at the corners of the hearth.

Sescnen was not a wealthy man, a small Chieftain, but his Household nonetheless held three Druids, Magicians, Counsellors, and Men of Judgment. The springing candle flames showed the chief of these plucking at the elbow of his master, whispering in hostility and suspicion, his eyes angry on the tired man beside the dying turf glow.

But Sescnen set him aside, and looked a long moment at Patrick, as though there was something that must be decided between them. Then he moved slowly forward and laid his graying head on Patrick's breast in the ancient, honored gesture of submission and respect.

"Adze head is come," he said, and above his bent head Patrick looked at the silent household and the angry Druid, and lifted his hand in the sign of the Cross.

24

Beside his father, the boy Benet sighed and moved closer to the priest, and the troubled look of the early day had left his face. As his father drew back, he edged up close to Patrick.

"What do we call you," he asked, "if we wished to speak with you?"

The man looked down at the child, kindness on his tired face.

"You may call me Father," he said gently, and Benet's eyebrows drew together and he glanced with questioning face at his father behind him.

"I am your father in God," Patrick said to him then, and the child looked at him as if he did not understand, but for the moment was willing to set it aside for something more important.

"Tell me then—Father—" He came out with the question that had been troubling him all evening, through all the long preaching that had brought the first word of God to the men of Erin. "Tell me then, Father—when you got out of the boat down on the Strand of the Shallows, why did you not wade ashore like all the other men? Why did this one," he pointed to the biggest man of the group of strangers, "why did this one have to carry you to the land?"

Several of Patrick's followers looked shocked, and from across the fire Finola moved as if she would rebuke her son, but the tired, weatherbeaten face of the priest crumpled into a smile as innocent and simple as Benet's own.

"Why, my son," he said, and laid a hand on the boy's shoulder, "that is simply answered! I do not like to get my feet wet!"

Benet laughed aloud, and looked all around for everyone to share his joke, and the Roman priest laughed with him, cheerfully, and in a moment the fire was ringed with smiling faces, and the jest was repeated all down through the Hall and out along the dark hill of the dun, and the small simplicity pleased the people, warming them to the priest, and leaving them more willing to listen to all he said.

But Macha had moved out of the ring of candlelight, and paid no heed to the small joke, leaning against the plaster wall in a sudden misery of weariness that had overtaken her as she listened to the tired yet overwhelming voice telling of this new God. All her bright certainty in her future was suddenly vanished and there was only confusion to take its place. As Patrick and his companions passed her, she looked at them in something like despair. She knew a spell had taken her as she listened, and she knew a deep, almost fearful certainty that had no reason in it, that what this man said was truth. But there was Tara, and her parents, and a new husband, and all the things she had been sure of before; all her life of learning at the feet of the Druids.

She looked after the back of the Roman as he left the Hall to go to his Guest House, and knew the same feeling as when Benet had shouted at his father in the dusk. Nothing was ever going to be the same again.

Chapter Three

The next morning Macha woke early, in the high-built bower where she slept with her foster sisters, and she lay a few moments while sleep drifted away. But wakefulness came quickly in the bright light and the high, cool air, and with it the clear memory of the man who had preached the night before. Thinking of him, she could no longer lie in peace; anxious lest he might be gone with the breaking day, before she had seen him again. Finola had told her that he and his friends would not be staying in the household, having put into the river mouth only to beg food and water and rest before going on farther north to the Kingdom of Ulidia, where the man Patrick had friends from the days of his captivity, and where he planned to start his mission.

Dawn was not long past when she crept out of the sleeping place, and the light was still only on the hilltops, the low sun a bright path on the gray early calm of the sea. No one was yet about, save the guards, and the frail threads of turf smoke from the damped-down fires rose straight into the windless air. On the small, narrow path from the well, Benet came up beside her like a shadow. He looked pale and tired as if he had not slept.

"You are early, Macha, my sister."

"And you."

They looked at each other in the still, cool light, and both knew why they were about at this hour; both of them caught and held by the strange fascination of the man from the sea. But they were shy as yet of what they felt, and unwilling to put it into words. In silence they walked a little through the paths of the dun, and although neither of them would speak of it, both pairs of eyes were on the thatched roof of the Guest House, on the lower slope of the dun, behind the grass-grown walls of its own small rath.

Macha's feet trailed slowly to a halt. At last she turned her quiet, puzzled face to the boy beside her, and she looked far from the tempestuous girl who had danced so gaily in the edges of the sea.

"Did you think he spoke the truth, Benet?" she asked urgently. A small wind was rising to bother the still morning; the smoke threads flickered and the air was cold on her hands. "Did you think he spoke the truth? The one with the adze head? Have we really not known the true God, but wandered in darkness as he said, led into false worship by the Druids?"

28

She was desperately confused, unable to sort out in her mind the things the man had said, and the spell and fascination of the Roman himself, with his apologetic smile and his clear compelling voice.

"He's very handsome," she said suddenly.

Benet left this, and answered her question.

"I believe he spoke truth," he said, and again his boy's face looked older than its years, but this time set in serenity and content. The girl watched him curiously, knowing him to be as spellbound by Patrick as she was herself, but she had the feeling that the boy understood more, even though he was younger. "I believe," he said again. "And the Druids know he tells the truth, and they are frightened. Adze head will come, they said. Now Adze head is here. The prophecy is fulfilled, and we are part of it."

He spoke the last words as if to himself, and fascinated they stood together and stared down at the Guest-House roof, as if they might learn something of the mystery simply by knowing that Patrick lay beneath it. Here and there the first people began to come from the huts and dwellings about the business of the day, moving over the long, green slopes of the dun. With the rekindling of fires, the turf smell drifted sharp and sweet along the wind, and far below them the cattle threaded their way out to the pastures from the safety of their pens.

Benet took her hand.

"We'll go down to the Guest House. It's just possible we may be able to see him, even if we cannot speak." His voice was urgent, as though even this much was desperately necessary to him.

Inside the gates, the Household of the priests was all astir, but they moved about the tasks of early day in silence, stepping carefully and glancing around at any noise. As the boy and girl pushed open the high wooden gates in the grass-grown wall, the big man who had lifted Patrick from the boat rushed forward and held his finger to his lips, urging them to quietness.

"This is no time to come here," he hissed at them. "Our Father rests, and we must wake him soon for Prime. Leave him in peace."

Macha would have turned and gone, but Benet moved purposefully around the big man as though he knew he need not heed him.

"We will not disturb the Father," he said. "Oh, why does he sleep here?"

The girl followed him, with a doubtful look at the protesting giant, and then stopped as he had done, to stare in surprise. Around the circular dwelling where he housed his guests, Sescnen had created a small garden, so that they might walk in peace and shelter in the shade of trees, and take their ease above the sea. Here on the young grass, the Roman lay asleep. About him, the members of his Household in their white robes looked in anger and indignation at the two young people, and gestured them to silence.

"But why here?" whispered Macha, and gazed at him with sudden compassion, a tired man with his hair awry, and no flashing blade of prophecy around his brow.

"He was up long since," the man said beside her. "Up long since, and his Mass said. But our voyage was tedious and he is still tired. When he sat here a moment, sleep took him again."

Benet stood there on the grass in silence, as though he were alone, his rapt eyes never leaving the brown, sleeping face. Suddenly he stirred, and bending to the fragrant beds, he picked fistfuls of the sweet-smelling primroses and violets and the wild blue tangle of forget-me-nots. Pushing his way between the watching men, he fell to his knees and laid them gently on the breast of the sleeping Patrick.

"Foolish child, come away!"

"Leave him in peace, boy."

"Go away, child."

Their angry scolding did what Benet's gentle gesture had failed to do. Patrick's eyes opened and looked up at the group around him, the young boy kneeling with his eyes fixed on his and the torn fragments of flowers still between his fingers; the angry faces of his followers and the nervous girl waiting for him to be as furious as all the other men. But the priest only smiled his odd, diffident smile and sat up gathering the flowers into his hands. He looked long and steadily then at the boy, who had never taken his eyes off his.

"Trouble him not," he said then, incomprehensibly, and the men about him stared at the boy. "Trouble him not, for he shall be the heir to my Kingdom." And the men listened and did not understand, and Patrick and the boy looked at each other long and quietly, but only Patrick looked into the future, to Benet's own Bishopric, when he would indeed inherit his new master's kingdom.

Macha was as puzzled as all the men.

"What did he mean by that?" she asked Benet irritably, as later in the day they walked again for a while beside the sea. It had been difficult to get him by himself, for now he clung to Patrick like a shadow. "What did he mean?"

"The future will tell," Benet answered equably. "The future will tell. I only know now that I will follow him wherever he goes. He will be my life, he and the God he teaches."

"And your parents?" she asked jealously.

"They are willing. Especially my father."

Macha's brows drew down. She felt confused and cheated, having still got all in the world that she had had yesterday, but doubtful suddenly whether it was of any real value, since she had listened to this calm, compelling voice that told her of a new God and a new world. Benet's serene face added to her irritation, for it seemed as if he had settled all the doubts he had spoken of the day before,

31

and for her, doubt had only just begun; nor did she understand it. She said so, kicking at the sand with a restless foot.

"I don't understand," she cried furiously. "I don't understand. Yesterday you said your future was like a cloud with nothing in it, but today suddenly you know everything, and are content! Does it all lie in one man?"

The boy turned and looked at her and gave a small shrug, as if he could not hope to explain.

"It all lies in one man," he agreed. "And in one God. Today the cloud has cleared, and I have a future."

"And I have not," she cried despairingly. "I have not! He has come, this Adze head and given you a future, but he has taken mine away. Why did he not stay where he was! We were well enough without him. Yesterday, I was happy!"

She stamped with fury, forgetting where she was, and under her angry feet the wet sand slid away and toppled her, so that she sat down and stayed there, with her head upon her knees, weeping angrily in the cold sea.

Benet watched a moment helplessly, and then he turned and left her, going back to Patrick.

Chapter Four

"There is news of him! There is news of him!" Benet flung
open the door of his sisters' grianin, and the skin curtains
shook and clattered on their poles in the urgency of his
coming. Macha looked up and her hands fell still above the
silks of her embroidery. There was no need to ask the boy
of whom he spoke, with the news bright in his face, and the
very curls of his hair alive with excitement. The girl sighed.
Patrick and his company had sailed away two days after

33

they had come, and though she knew it to be foolish, she had hoped that that would be the end of them. She had hoped to push Patrick and his God out of her mind and forget them, slipping back into the happy groove where her life had always rested. The days had slipped past and spring had warmed into early summer, and she had begun to think that this had come about, for now they had been gone fifteen days and there was no news of them. A few days more and her father would be coming for her from the Hill of Tara, and then her life would go on exactly as he had planned, and she need decide nothing for herself.

Now she looked up at the boy, flushed and panting in the doorway, with the gray of a windswept sea behind his head, and the seagulls crying mournfully in the dark air. She didn't want to hear his news, and yet she could not bear it if she didn't.

"Benet, son," his mother said. "That is no way to come into your mother's bower. News of whom?"

Benet looked at her with as near impatience as his mild face could ever muster.

"Oh, my mother! The Roman! Patrick!"

Macha watched him in silence, and his mother laid down her needlework and looked at him, too, and the light faded from Benet's eyes. Macha turned from one face to the other and could not bear the sadness of the mother's look.

"And now, Benet?" Finola said at last.

Benet did not take his eyes from hers and his face was clouded with love and grief, but he stood straight and quiet with the same steadfast look as the man with the adze head blazing in the firelight over his brow.

"And now, my mother." He moved to pick up for her a tangle of silks that had slithered from her work, and laid them back into her lap. "And now, my mother, now that I know where he is, I will follow him. My father said I might," he added defensively at her instinctive gesture of protest.

There was silence in the shadowed room. The seagulls cried above the thatch, and Finola picked up her embroidery.

"I said you might, too, my son," she said calmly, but she did not lift her head. They feel it, too, thought Macha, this spell the Roman casts! They feel it, too, that they are willing to give him Benet! She did not feel herself quite so strange and lost, to know that Patrick had won over two such wise and quiet people as Sescnen and his wife.

"Tell us your news of him," Finola said then.

The boy needed no bidding. He flung himself on the skins at his mother's feet, turning his eager face from her to Macha as he told his story.

"He is gone to the north! To the Kingdom of Ulidia to a place by the borders of a landlocked sea. They hid their boat when they were arrived, and Patrick went alone to seek the Chief, but a swineherd had seen them and gave warning, so that the Chief came raging down the hill of his dun in anger, ready to attack Patrick with his spears and his two savage wolfhounds!" His horror was echoed on Macha's face, but the mother stayed calm. "From where they hid, his followers could see him, and they flung themselves on their knees and prayed to their God, for they thought Patrick certain to meet his death either from the spears or the dogs, for he carried nothing but his staff! But listen! Listen to this!" He knelt up and laid his hands among the bright silks in her lap, willing her to his own amazement, turning to Macha to draw her in too.

"As the two men met," he went on slowly and importantly, "the watchers saw Patrick go forward at once and lay his hand on the head of the most savage dog, and it nuzzled him and reached to lick his face! Then Dichu, the Chief, unlooped his spear and laid it aside, and greeted Patrick with kindness! Do you not see, my mother? It was an answer to their prayer! The hand of his God was lifted

35

to save Patrick, who could not save himself against the dogs or the spear!"

Finola lifted her head and looked at him and her eyes were wise and gentle.

"I think, my son," she said with a small smile, "it is more that this man Dichu is wedded to the daughter of Patrick's old master from the days of his slavery. That is why he sought him out. Also," her voice was dry, "also, he has a good hand with a dog. He told us that the boat in which he fled to Gaul held a cargo of wolfhounds. After that voyage, one dog would be nothing!"

She looked kindly at the boy's crestfallen face.

"Do not think, Benet, that I make less of Patrick when I smile at these wild stories. There will be many more of them, I am sure." She laid aside her needle and faced him. "He did know of Dichu, my son," she said. "And he does have a way with dogs. But more than either of these things, that peaceful meeting would have come about because Dichu would have looked at Patrick, and seen as we did, a steadfast, decent man. And Dichu is a brave and honest man himself, so they would have liked each other on sight. There is no need, my Benet, to seek the wild and strange when trying to tell of what the Roman does. He does not need the magic of the Druids. Your father and I are sure that he will capture Erin for his God, but he will do it as he has captured us; with simple goodness, you will see. It has been long foretold that such a man would come to Erin, and that Erin would be his. We see him here, my son, and we see him honest and simple, and that is why we let you go to him."

Macha listened, and struggled to sort her feelings, jealous that Benet should have everything made easy for him. If she could go and hear more, and listen longer to the Roman teaching, then she, too, might understand more. Was this

God of Patrick like so many other things, only for the men and boys?

Benet had paused a moment, thinking on what his mother said, and then he clearly set it aside to think of again, and rushed on with his tale.

"Well, whatever fostered it, Patrick and the Chieftain Dichu became at once fast friends, and Dichu took them all straight away to his mighty dun. Nearby he has given them a barn, a huge barn, to use as a church. That is what they call the place where they say the Mass, which is the worship of their God. All this a man told me who has come from him! The first Church of God, my mother, in the land of Erin!"

He fell silent then, and his eyes were wide and distant on something he alone could see; perhaps the barn of Dichu, on the green distant hill above the Lough of Strangford, with the new faithful coming one by one to the unfamiliar Mass. His mother watched him a long moment and then stood up swiftly and left the room, and he did not see her go. His eyes fell then on Macha, and they stared at each other long and wide-eyed, taken by the same spell.

Through all the long gray day she was silent and thoughtful, watching all the preparations through the dun for the journey of the Chieftain's son, and the company that would go with him. It was large, for many of Sescnen's people had, like Macha, been stirred and shaken by the preaching of the Roman, and could not settle again to their fishing and their fields until they had found him again, and heard more of the things he taught. Men, women, and children would be walking behind Benet on his journey through the mild weather to learn more of God.

It was not until they were seated at dinner in the evening that she spoke, and she did it suddenly, as if on the instant she had made up her mind.

37

"Benet," she said urgently, and leaned toward him under the cover of the harpist at the fire. "Benet."

The boy turned to her, his face serene with the happiness of the next morning when he would set out on his longed-for journey.

"Benet! I am coming with you tomorrow!"

He turned so sharply that the ale ran from his tumbled cup and spread in a small river across the board, dripping to the rushes on the floor. Frantically he pulled himself together and looked around to see that no one else had heard her, and then turned back with a sudden hopeful idea.

"You don't mean," he whispered, "that you are being allowed to go?"

She shook her head, and he stared at her appalled.

"I'll talk to you outside after the meal," he whispered, conscious of his mother's eyes on them, but it was dark night before they walked on the ridge of the hill, having slipped out as the chess sets were being placed on the tables and the Hall settled to its evening pleasures. On the hill across the valley to the west, points of light flickered in the Grove of the Sacred Oaks, where Coran and his followers sought desperate auguries of fear and death, to lay a blight on the journey in the morning.

"Macha, you cannot do it!"

"I *am* doing it."

Her voice was a little tired and stiff with obstinacy. She had said this so often since they crept from the Hall. She knew it to be wrong, but she was going to do it. Like so many others, drawn by the fascination of Patrick and the words he preached; she could not settle again to her own life. She must follow him and try to understand.

"But Macha." Benet spoke despairingly beside her. "Won't you understand! You are foster child to my father. If you run away, what of him?"

"What of your father?" Now she was rough and defensive, touched on the one thing that terrified and upset her. Her own parents she hardly knew, but she turned her mind from the grief and actual danger that she would bring to Sescnen and Finola by her action, and she did not want Benet to remind her of it. "What of him?" She pretended that she didn't know.

"It could mean his death, and all the family, too, and the destruction of the dun!" She heard his voice rising in misery, echoing her own fears, but she refused to heed it.

"Oh no, Benet! You talk foolishly!"

He pleaded, holding to her sleeve.

"Yes Macha, yes! Your father would have every right to take this dun with fire and the sword, and what chance would my father have. Your father is of the Household of the High King! To offend him is to offend the King, and it would be a matter for the Avenger of Insults, with all the High King's Warriors behind him."

Bleakly, Macha knew it to be true, even if she would not admit it. She looked in darkness along the ridge of the hill with the sheen of the sea beyond it, and saw the glow of light that rose in the dark sky above the fires and torch-light of the dwellings of the dun. In her mind she saw that soft glow turned to rolling scarlet above the crackling flames, with the gentle Sescnen and his family dead in their burning home.

"No!" she shouted fiercely at Benet, angry with him to ease her own feelings. "No! My father would not do it! He is a judge, a just man! He would know your father had no part in it if I ran away; that I would do it myself alone! He would be angry with me, no more. He would not do it, Benet!"

"I should tell my father," he said somberly. "But I won't. You do whatever you like, and I understand what you do, because I cannot help following him either. But it's not for you, and I want nothing to do with it. You cannot come with me."

A watchlight flared on the ridge of the dun, and lit his determined, disapproving face and caught gold lights from the collar around his neck. Macha looked at him in the sudden light, loving him and hating him in the same moment.

"I don't *want* to come with you! You will not even know me in the crowd." She was on the edge of tears. She had thought that Benet would understand and help her, but it seemed that this God of Patrick was as she feared. As far as she was concerned, he was only for the men and boys.

Benet turned away from her and then as suddenly turned back, and she felt his hard young arms go around her in a sharp, fierce hug.

"Macha, sweet sister, forgive me for being so angry." He let her go and she heard him sigh. "I would do anything for you—but there is my father—and I know what this will cost him. But don't tell me any more about it, and I won't know of it. Then you can do as you want."

She wept then, and turned from him to run away into the darkness, torn with misery over the trouble she must cause, but utterly unshaken in her determination to follow the Man of God.

"And it is not," she told herself fiercely as she ran, for she had heard this said of some of the women, "simply that he has a handsome face and a voice of gold. It is his God I want to know."

The clothes were easy. Many of the household chests were kept in the grianin, and here all the bright garments of Sescnen's boyhood had been stored, waiting for his son. Tears and misery came again in the silent darkness, when she hacked at her long red plait and held it at last in her hand, as though she had in that one act cut off all her happy childhood and her safety for the sake of something she longed for, but feared not a little, and did not understand.

The company left for Ulidia in the morning as the first flat rays of the sun striped the level sea, and dawn crept through the Grove of the Sacred Oak to light the cold, defeated faces of the Druids. No one, least of all Benet, took particular note of the young lad who walked alone, with the hood of his gray frieze cloak gathered around his neck to hide the ragged edges of his hair.

Chapter Five

The great Spring Festival was over in the Palace of the High King at Tara, and all the guests had ridden away. Only the still vast Household of Leary, the High King himself, remained within the encircling walls that gleamed like a beacon to travelers still two days journey off across the flat, rolling plains of Meath.

In the peace and quiet after weeks of feasting and ceremonies and games, happy preparation was being made in the homestead of the Chief Judge, against the homecoming of his eldest daughter.

"That is good," said Macha's mother, and nodded contentedly as she watched the bondmaid spread the bed with fresh sheets of snow-white linen, newly bleached on the drying-grounds beside the river. "That is good, Kathlend. And the new curtains—you have them up?" Labran of the Long Memory was a man of wealth and taste, and in spite of the laws of fosterage that laid down the standards of Macha's life with Sescnen, she would come home to fine surroundings such as she had never known in the wind-swept dun beside the Western Sea. It was more the custom for sons to be sent out to fosterage, but Sescnen had been anxious for the honor of fostering a child of his illustrious kinsman, and there had been no more sons. Now it filled Bres with happiness bright as the Spring day to think of having the girl back again, and all her daughters gathered around her if only for a little time.

"She will be pleased with it, I think," she said to the bondwoman, and then sighed, almost sad that she could do no more. She came out through the big sunny grianin and down the steep stairs to sit awhile in the sloping garden and watch for her husband coming to his evening meal.

The Rath of Labran lay, like all those of the senior members of the High King's Household, close inside the outer walls of Tara on the low slopes of the Hill, set in fair land of its own, and with wide acres beyond the walls for pasture and cultivation. From where Bres sat, she could see the whole long, green sweep of the Hill of Tara, crowned against the mild sky with all the vast buildings that were the home of the High King of Erin. Long before he saw her, and lifted a hand in distant greeting, she could see her husband, walking slowly down the green evening Hill, followed by his servants, his clothes bright with the colors of his high rank. He walked with the light step of his alert good humor, pleased with his world, his head up to the soft air of the evening. She smiled and lost sight of him as he drew close to the Rath, but she waited where she sat, knowing his habits, and it was not long before he arrived beside her, followed by a bondman bearing a deep silver cup of mead.

He took it and drained it dry before he spoke, breathing out a long breath of content. "Ah, that was most welcome! Leary, our King, was very kingly today, and a trial to the patience. I am tired."

His wife smiled at him again and patted the stone seat beside her with a welcoming hand, the gold bracelets clinking heavy on her wrists.

"He was not our dear cousin Leary, then, today?" She was well familiar with the changing moods of the High King, at one moment their amiable kinsman, and at the next their monarch, remote and untouchable as the stars beyond the mountains.

"No." Labran passed a hand across his face, and his wrist gleamed with deep bracelets of fine-worked gold. Slowly he relaxed beside Bres. "No. He was very much a king today, and took a lot of my time, and I had much to do as I am traveling tomorrow to bring Macha from the dun of Sescnen." His long, intelligent face grew soft, and a smile touched the corners of his wide mouth. "It will be good to have her here with us again. The last time we were with her, I thought her to be growing very fair."

Bres looked at her husband, and thought that not only Leary the King had two faces and two sides to his nature. How many of the evil doers who were brought before the severe and stern-faced judge in the Rath of the Druids would recognize this soft-hearted and humorous man who so doted on his children.

"Do you think we have chosen well for her?" she asked him, and Labran looked at her.

44

"Chosen well for her?" he asked. "Oh, you speak of her husband. Yes, Bres my wife, I am sure we have chosen well for her. Kiann of the Bright Axe. He is everything she should be honored to find in a husband; kinsman to the King himself, one of the mightiest warriors in the army, indeed a Champion of the Collar, and Avenger of Insults to the High King." He smiled a little. "And," he added, "he has enough knowledge of the tales and history of his land to please even me. Oh, he is well chosen, I think. She should be content with him. We do not want her driving her cows back round the hill, forsaking his dun when a couple of seasons are past. Sescnen tells me she has grown to a high spirit."

Bres looked shocked, and peered into his face to see if he really meant what he said.

"You jest," she said, relieved. "Of course she will be content with him. We will see her children, and perhaps even the children of her children. We are young yet ourselves." Her face was gentle at the thought of her absent daughter and the fine young warrior who was to be her husband. He was tall, too.

"He will be almost two hands taller than she is," she murmured. "That will be good. It is pleasing for a girl to be smaller than her husband."

Labran's thick, fair eyebrows twitched and he laid a hand on hers.

"Yes," he said. "These things matter to you women. I cannot think how you are wed to one so undersized and ugly as I am."

She smiled herself at that, and shook his hand a little about her own, and they sat together in silence and content, looking with pleased certainty into the future they had planned for their daughter.

It was dark and the family gathered for the evening meal when Sescnen came. Through the warm hum of talk and laughter in the Hall, the urgent rumble of chariot wheels thundered in the quiet evening along the stone-built roads through Tara, and the high flare of torches threw their scarlet glare against the windows.

"A curse on hospitality," grumbled Labran as he heard the commotion beyond his doors. "Who is it that I must entertain at this hour?"

Bres shushed him and yet smiled a little, and from their own tables his children looked at him in shocked delight. Their father made a face at them, thrusting out his lower lip.

"I am content as I am for tonight," he said. "Shush me not, good wife." He stretched his bare feet along the couch where he lay to eat, shifting the small yellow cat that purred against his ankles. "I am tired and warm, and the food is good, and I looked forward to some music from my children when I am full. A curse again, I say, on hospitality."

His eyes rested amused again on his little daughters, taking pleasure in their small grinning faces that so delighted to hear their father mock the very rules on which their life was laid. And he a *judge!* But even as he spoke and looked with tenderness at their giggles, he laid down the piece of meat that he was eating, and signed to a servant to bind on his sandals so that he might go properly to meet his unexpected guest at the door of his Hall.

But Sescnen was too quick for him, striding with desperate urgency through the wide doors into the peace and warmth and firelight, with trouble written on his drawn face, and his own company anxious and appalled behind him.

Labran swung to his feet and came to him around the fire, stumbling a little on his sandal strings, the four tall candles flickering in the wind of his passing, and lighting the surprise on his face.

"Sescnen, my kinsman! Greetings to you, and the welcome of my house. May there be always meat and drink

46

for you, and land beyond your door." Despite his mischief with the children, he kept his curiosity in check until the rules of courtesy were honored and he had greeted Sescnen with a kiss on both cheeks and led him to the fire, and only the sharp flicker of his eyes on the face of the older man betrayed the questions that raced through his mind.

Bres had stood up, her feet bare in the rushes and the bright cushions of her couch tumbled to the floor unheeded. She knew trouble in this sudden visit and spoke before her husband, her soft voice sharp with fear.

"Macha," she said abruptly, and her hand went up to hold her throat, which seemed suddenly grown thick. Sescnen looked at her with his desperate eyes as the listening silence grew over the Hall behind him, for it made it easier to begin on this dreadful news that could mean war and death inside their tribe. His pale, gentle face was haggard with distress as he looked from one parent to the other, trying to find words to tell them. Down the long Hall the Household gathered close and the wild ones fingered their sword hilts and looked at each other hopefully with the light of pleasure in their eyes. Trouble over a foster child could lead to many a good battle, and life in Tara had been too still of late.

"Well," urged Labran when he did not speak. "Well, what of Macha?"

His mind was waiting to hear of the child's death. Children often died of fevers in the spring, and there would be no blame to Sescnen or his good wife. He stared in bewilderment when Sescnen answered, barely feeling the deep-drawn breath of relief from Bres at his side.

"She is *gone*, you say?" he repeated stupidly, and the fair, heavy brows drew down over his eyes. "What do you mean, she is gone?"

Anger was gathering in his strong face, and he stared at Sescnen in a new way. Once more Sescnen trembled at the trouble he must bring. In this homestead and in the whole Palace of Tara, life and belief were going on as they had gone on for more than any man's memory could count. How could he, a humble Chief, find words to tell the King's Brehon about the prophecy and the fulfillment of it; the coming of Adze head from the sea. And of the way the man had sat at his fireside, and stood in his fields, speaking such words of power and promise about a new world, that he had even been willing to give him his only son. Dumbly he lifted his hands in a hopeless gesture.

"Sescnen, my kinsman." Labran's voice was sharp. He was losing patience. "You are a guest in my house, and it is not proper that I show you anger, but I bid you speak at once and tell me of my child and what has happened to her. I do not have to remind you that she was your foster child, and of your duties to her according to the law. If she is alive, why is she outside your house?"

Helplessly Sescnen gathered his courage and began to speak, telling as best he could the whole strange story of the coming of Adze head from the sea with his companions, in fulfillment of the Druid prophecy, with their news of a new God. Bres stared at him wide-eyed when he said he had given Benet, and spoke through the growing amazement around the fire.

"You allowed this Roman to take Benet?" she asked him in wonder, and stared at her own eagerly listening children, for she knew what his only son had meant to Sescnen. The tired, frightened man looked back at her as though from her alone he might hope to get understanding of what had happened.

"I allowed Benet to follow him, when he had found a place to settle. I thought the man worthy of it." Bres gazed at his haggard face, bewildered and unable to find anger against some unknown force so great that it had driven Sescnen to part forever with the boy who was the joy of his life. But Labran did not reason in that way, and faced his kinsman with his fair face darkening with fury.

"And Macha?"

Sescnen shrugged helplessly.

"She was content in everything until this Roman came. I had told her she was to go home, and that her marriage was planned." Beside him, Bres gasped and her fingers flew to her mouth. In the anxiety about the child herself, she had for the moment forgotten to whom she had been offered in marriage. There was blood and war in this business, and no one could prevent it, and the poor gentle Sescnen, who would raise a hand to none, must take the burden of it all.

He was going on speaking, turning back defensively to the cold, accusing eyes of Labran.

"She was content, bright with happiness to come home, and pleased, I think, to face her marriage. But after this Roman priest had preached among us, she was like so many more of my people, confused and troubled, and desperate to hear more so that they might better understand the new ways he taught, and the new god he spoke of." He sighed, and looked from the furious father to the troubled mother.

"It never occurred to me," Sescnen went on, "that she would try to follow him. But that is where she must have gone. Yesterday morning, my son, Benet, and many of my people left for Ulidia, where Patrick is settled with the Chieftain Dichu, and she must have left with them. Although I bade my son farewell and watched them all go, I did not see her. When we could not find her, we searched for her everywhere, and an old woman came to Finola, my wife, an old woman who sews upon the household clothes since I myself was young, and knows them all. She told that in the crowd that left the dun, she saw a boy with red hair beneath his hood, and she was sure the clothes he wore were mine, long stored in chests until my son was grown. She thought him to be some poor lad to whom my wife had given these clothes for the journey. Now I know that it must have been Macha."

"And knowing her confused and sad over this man, should you not have watched her all the closer?" Labran's face was hard and cold, the face of the King's judge, and his voice was clipped.

Sescnen looked old and defeated, his very hair limp with his distress. He raised two hopeless pleading hands, and then closed them and let them drop.

"My son," he said. "My son was going." In those few painful words, Bres read all the grief and sadness that there must have been in that bright morning for him and for Finola, so that they neither saw nor thought of any other child except the brown-haired boy who was leaving them forever. She moved a step toward Sescnen, her face soft with pity, but Labran went on unmoved, concerned only with right and wrong.

"And where has she gone, you say?"

"To the dun of Dichu, on the shore of the inland sea which lies against the Western Sea itself, on the coast of Ulidia. Dichu has given the priest shelter and protection, and a great barn for a place for all to come and worship. He is a very powerful Chieftain."

Labran snorted and dug his hands inside his leather belt.

"I know of Dichu. And shelter and protection are what your Roman will need, my kinsman, by the time we reach him. Know you, Sescnen, what you have done in this?" He drew himself up and glared under his heavy brows at his unhappy cousin, and around the edges of the Hall the candles in their cressets flickered on the bright, hopeful faces of those who had fingered their swords. "I will tell you what you have done! You have neglected my child in fosterage, and so insulted me, and thus insulted the High King himself." Sescnen's eyes widened and Labran made a gesture of impatience. "You are but a small Chief, cousin, but you must know that an insult to the kinsman of the King inside his Household is an insult to the King himself! And he will avenge it! We will wipe this Roman who has stolen my daughter, and his henchman Dichu, off the green face of Erin, and that will be an end to this nonsense about a new god. We have long been expecting it," he added absently, and Sescnen's anxious eyes brightened a moment.

"There was an ancient prophecy by the Druids," he said eagerly, as if to prove that the whole thing was outside the power of a humble man such as he, but Labran snorted again and looked at him almost with contempt.

"It was not a difficult one, my poor Sescnen," he said. "Have we not known of this Roman religion for many, many seasons? Have we not heard of its power in the hot lands to the east? The Druids would be but poor creatures if they were not able to foresee that somebody, some day, would try to bring it over the Western Sea. There is no magic about this, my kinsman, but magic or not, there will be an end to it. The Elements have served us well and all our forefathers, and we'll not forsake them for any God of Rome. As for your part in this—"

There was silence in the Hall, and Sescnen stared at Labran in puzzlement, unable in this confused and frightened moment to think clearly of what he had said, or to sort out magical prophecy from common sense. Bres watched his white and weary face and pitied him, in spite of her own fears for her daughter. It must have been something far beyond himself that had led his usual quiet wisdom into this; something so great that it had driven him to part with Benet. She could not forget this, and moved a little toward Labran to beg him for pity. But she had no need. Labran was a just man, a judge in thought as well as deed.

"For your part," he went on, "we will wait and see what comes out of it all. Our daughter herself should have known better than to go, and if we get her safely back, then we may overlook the folly that did not watch her more closely." His voice grew gentler. "You are older than I am, Sescnen, my cousin, and I have no desire to destroy your life and your home, for till this moment your house has served my daughter well."

Sescnen did not speak, staring with bent head into the fire, overcome with sadness that there should be an end like this to all the happy years of Macha's life within his dun. His head jerked up at Labran's next words.

"But this does not rest with me alone, Sescnen. We have not told you to whom we are betrothing our daughter."

The older man shook his head, not seeing that it mattered.

"To Kiann of the Bright Axe." The last shreds of color drained from Sescnen's face. "Yes. The Avenger of Insults to the King." Labran could not resist a moment of satisfaction, bouncing a little on the balls of his feet, his thumbs hooked again in his leather belt. "A fine young fellow. And with being the bravest warrior in all Erin, he is as well versed in the tales and poems and history of his land as the King's Olaves themselves." He came back to the matter in hand, and now with the first shock of his anger past, and sound hope that the girl was safe, he looked almost in pity at the defeated man before him, and his voice grew gentle. "So let us all hope, Sescnen, that we can bring Macha safely back to her home, for Kiann will be avenging no vague insult to the King if she is harmed. He will be avenging his own bride, and the dun of Dichu, no matter how great, will flame into ashes above the head of this Roman from the sea, and the dun of Sescnen will surely follow it."

Sescnen said nothing, his mind on the thought that not only Macha was in the dun of Dichu. There was Benet also, but no one seemed to remember this.

"Unless all is well with the girl," went on Labran, "it will be with Kiann the Avenger you will have to parley. Now come with me, and we will lay the whole thing without delay before Leary himself."

Chapter Six

Darkness had fallen over the Hill of Tara; lit here and there
with the moving scarlet of a blaze of torchlight, and patched
with the soft gold of the haze of lamp and candlelight from
the homesteads on the lower slopes. From Labran's dwelling
it was a long walk up to the crest of the Hill, trying to
Sescnen's weary and nervous legs, and they walked in silence, followed by the company without which a man of
Labran's rank could never move into the presence of his
King. Never before, in his quiet, undemanding life, had

Sescnen set foot on the holy Hill, but he had no eyes now to look at the spreading, mist-crowned spaces, bulked with the darkness of raths, and bright with the lights and voices of those who lived behind them. He had no eyes for the evening silence of the empty schools, where through the days students crowded to studies of law and history and medicine and geography, and the ancient art of being a King's warrior. He could only look up with sick despair as they breasted the last slope of the Hill, bitterly conscious that between him and the warm lights of the King was the dark, desperate mound of the Rath of the Hostages, where lay the prisoned enemies of the King, pledging him to safety.

They stood at last before the gate of Caher Crofin, the King's house, and Sescnen's knees were weak with weariness and fear, but as Labran's servants spoke with the Keeper of the Door, even his anxious eyes could not but notice the richness of the great carved door pillars that reared above his head, threaded in the torchlight with the gleam of bronze and gold. The Keeper was unwilling to let them in, standing firm between his two young guardian warriors, who leaned on the silken loops of their spears, their faces in the shadow and their long formal curls hazed by the blaze of light behind them in the court.

"It is evening," the Keeper said. "The King has had his meal, and now he rests."

"Our master bids us say that it is urgent."

"Tell your master that he should come back in the morning."

Although Labran stood immediately behind his servants, and was long and deeply friendly with the Keeper of the Door, he could not speak to him directly when he came as he did now, on the King's business.

The servant turned to relay the message, and he gave him a little push.

"Tell the Keeper," he said loudly and clearly that his

voice might carry, "that I, Labran of the Long Memory, Chief Brehon to the High King, say that it is urgent. Even knowing the King's ways as I do, and that in the evening he would rest, I say that I must see him at once."

Across the servants' heads, he looked at the Keeper, with the lights of the court falling clear on his face, and drove the urgency of his message. A night of delay might lose him his child. Who knew what dangers she might be led into by this madman from the sea, who had coaxed her away from Sescnen by some spell—not magic as his poor cousin thought, but some force, nevertheless too big for her to understand. The man at the door made up his mind.

"Let it be so," he said grudgingly, and motioned the two warriors aside. As Labran passed him between the rasp of the grounding spears, he put formality aside and spoke to him direct, shaking his head. "No blame to me, Labran my friend, if you do not like the welcome you get from him. Not even his dinner has mellowed him tonight. He has had a long day and needs his rest."

Labran laid a hand on his arm.

"No blame to you, my friend, no matter how he treats me." He smiled a moment at the doubtful face. "I have shared his day, and I am weary too, but this business will not wait."

The man nodded, and turned to a servant, bidding him go ahead to the High King and tell him that Labran waited and asked to speak with him.

In the Hall of the High King there were no shadows beyond the firelight and the candlelight, as in the humble dun of Sescnen. The whole immense circular Hall blazed with the light of lamps hanging in their rows from the painted beams of the ceiling, their soft light falling on the murmuring company of the household.

Beyond the second fire stood the royal table, and behind it a magnificent carved chair, before which the King's huge

55

candle burned through night and day; always by his hearth fire if he was in his palace, and before his tent if he went forth to war. Warm skins were thrown above the rushes on the floor, and the couches that stood about on it were rich and bright with thickly padded cushions; the pillars of the sleeping rooms, and the poles of their curtains were bright with enamel and the sheen of gold.

For a moment, Sescnen almost forgot his anxiety and distress, staring around him, astonished at the light and brilliance and the cheerful hum of conversation from the Household, dressed in all the gay, mixed colors of their high nobility. But the high-backed chair behind the fire was empty, and as they made their way up the Hall, it was clear that even the nobles closest to the King were all at ease, relaxed above their chessboards with ale cups at their sides; and the five guardian warriors who walked always at Leary's side were playing with Tossing Stones for wagers, on the floor.

"He is retired to his grianin." A man looked up as Labran passed. His long dark curls fell sleek down the checkered silk of his shirt, and the fingers on his chessmen were heavy with gold rings. "He wants none of us tonight. Only Fergus, and their perpetual war." He turned back to his board with a sharp, good-natured curse as his opponent took his Queen, and Labran passed on up the room. Then in a few moments he turned to Sescnen.

"We can go no further," he said. "Unless the King invites us."

"But where is he?" Sescnen ventured.

The servant who had preceded them appeared again as if from nowhere.

"The High King Leary will receive you," he said, bowing before Labran, but his face suggested they would be wiser not to accept the invitation. Sescnen was bewildered and nervous that everyone seemed to walk in terror of this King.

"Come, cousin," said Labran, and with difficulty he stiffened his knees to dignity and followed him up the wooden ladder to the grianin.

It was not as bad as all the warnings had led them to believe. Leary stared at them with expressionless eyes across the enameled beauty of his chessmen, and turned away from Fergus the Chess Player, who, on the other side of the table spent his whole life concocting moves to try and challenge the skill and cunning of his clever King. He listened in silence and stillness to the story told to him by Labran, only his blue, penetrating gaze moving from him to consider the unhappy face of Sescnen, and then back again to listen to what he said.

The judge stopped at last, having come to an end of all he had to say, but still the High King did not speak, continuing to look at him steadily with deep thoughtful eyes, but Labran knew him well and was not perturbed. He knew Leary to be thinking of all aspects of what he had heard before he would begin to speak on it, as was always his custom. Across the ivory board, in the silence, the brooding eyes of Fergus looked sadly at his chessmen and the point of peril to which he had brought his King, and he buried his thin hands in his sleeves and sighed bitterly to think that the game might have no end.

"There was a prophecy," Leary said then, sharply, and sat up on the edge of his couch, his bare feet dangling and his ringed hands on his knees. "There was a prophecy. I have no memory of it in words, but the Druids knew that this man would come. There was a prophecy."

Before him, in the soft light, Sescnen looked in bewilderment at Labran, who looked back at him and raised his eyebrows with an imperceptible shrug. Sescnen had waited through these last hours for the thunder of anger that must hit him for the personal insult to a member of the King's Household, and the rage that, in spite of Labran's protection, could have meant his death before they even found if the girl was safe. Instead, the High King had barely glanced at him, all his absorption with the man Patrick. Now Labran nudged his cousin openly. "The prophecy!" he hissed.

Sescnen stilled his trembling hands by clasping them together in a gesture of respect.

"If my King will permit me to speak." His dry throat brought him to a halt, and the sharp blue eyes shot him one single glance.

"I did not forbid you."

"No." He licked his lips. "My King, I know the prophecy."

The eyes waited.

"Adze head is come," he began, almost in a whisper, but as he spoke, he began to remember the strange, fulfilling quality of the spring dusk in which the man Patrick had landed on the Strand of the Shallows, and the steadfast, quiet strength of the man himself, and the words he spoke to fill the darkening hall of his quiet dun. His conviction strengthened his own voice, and by the time he reached the end of the prophecy and cried, "Amen, Amen!," his words rang with strength through the King's room, so that Fergus the Chess Player raised his head and stared at him in astonishment, stirred for one startled moment from his small private world of Queens and pawns and checkered squares. And in the bright, crowded hall below them, heads were raised all around the tables, and amazed faces stared up at the wide window of the King.

"Send me my Druids!" Leary lifted his feet and snapped his fingers for his sandals, and from a corner of the small room a servant fled to do his bidding. He did not cast another glance at Sescnen, who stood in the silence that followed his brave, uplifted words, waiting to know again if he was to hear of his own death.

Leary seemed to have forgotten him, clicking his long, ringed fingers impatiently as the servant knelt to tie the strings of his shoes, and looking up almost in surprise when Labran spoke to him.

"Leary, my cousin," he said. He ventured the more familiar address as there had been no explosions from the high tempered King; indeed he seemed vague and abstracted, concerned only with the story of the Roman priest. "Leary, my cousin, there is the matter of my daughter, that lies between me and my kinsman here."

He did not understand Leary at this moment. At another time, he would have burned with fury over the lightest insult, direct or indirect, ordering out Kiann and his warriors for the instant killing of one who had dared to deface his name. Now he looked at Labran almost as if he did not see him.

"He is nothing," he said, and did not even glance at Sescnen. "He is nothing. But stay with me and we will settle your revenge along with other more important things." He strode out of the grianin and went down the ladder into his Hall, his guardian warriors moving around him, dropping their Stones and looping their spears about their wrists.

Lucru the Druid was annoyed by the summons to his King. Like Labran, he had been tried and harassed through a long day by Leary's uncertain temper, and he was little disposed to be brought now from his evening rest to suffer more of it.

"You wanted me, my King?" He was short, peering at Leary with tired eyes from under the fringes of his hair, shaved over his crown into the disc of the sun. "You wanted me?" Of all his Household, Lucru alone could be brief and terse with the King and not be in danger of a ready death. Leary depended on him and on his learning and magic, and on his medicine if any of his royal family might fall sick. Leary depended on him and believed in him, and Lucru, who was a small man in his mind, preyed on this and did not give him the honor he deserved.

59

Leary sat forward now with his hands on the carved arms of his chair. The King's candle lighted his long, intelligent face, and brought gold lights into the heavy ringlets that fell about his cheeks.

"I wanted you," he said. "I wanted you to tell me of a prophecy of a man coming from the sea, with the telling of a new God, and a blade of gold above his brow. You know of it, for you have told me."

Lucru's irritation vanished, and a look almost of fear crept over his sallow face as he turned and looked at Lucran, his fellow Druid, beside him, and for a moment they stood thus, as though considering together something they had long feared. Lucru turned back to the King.

"We know of it, oh, Leary. We know of it." Slowly, as though the words were forced reluctantly out of him, he repeated the prophecy that Sescnen had shouted to his child through the dusk, with the strangers already on the shore. But on the lips of Lucru, it sounded like a threat, and not like the promise of wonder and blessing that it had seemed from Sescnen.

Leary listened to him and watched his pale face.

"And do you believe it?" he asked, when the Druid had finished, but he could hear no answer through the hum of astonishment and speculation that had risen around the tables, chessmen and needlework forgotten, and thrown Stones lost among the rushes. Impatiently the High King seized his Chain of Silence, and the sharp, insistent tinkle of the small gold bells filled the huge round chamber and brought the humming talk to silence.

"Do you believe it?" he asked again, and Lucru the Druid looked suddenly weary.

"There is more to it, oh my King," he said. "There is more to the prophecy."

"Yes?"

Lucru looked straight at his King, and Sescnen moved a little closer and forgot his own dangers.

"It says," said Lucru. "It says, 'When therefore all these things are come to pass, our Kingdom, which is a heathen one, will not be allowed to stand.'"

Now there was no need to ring the Chain of Golden Bells for silence. It was deep over the whole Hall, and startled faces turned to stare at each other above the forgotten games, and all the vast round chamber seemed filled with the loud breathing of the King.

Beside his chair, Labran's clever face was sharp and watchful, thinking rapidly over what he had said to Sescnen almost without thought, in a moment of angry contempt for his simplicity. Not only had the Druids foreseen, with logic and sense, and with no help from magic, that the teachers would inevitably come from the Church of Rome. They had also foreseen clearly that the Kingdom of Erin would not in the end resist them if they came.

Leary the King was not far behind him in his thoughts. He did not look again at Lucru, who eyed him with a certain sour satisfaction above his clasped hands of respect. He turned to Labran, close to him in the heat of the great candle.

"I claim myself insulted," he said clearly and formally, "by the insult offered to you, my kinsman, and within my Household. I am strongly urged to kill this man who has so treated you, and the dun that shelters him shall be destroyed. I shall deal red slaughter among them. In my name, you will go to my Champion, Kiann of the Bright Axe, and demand the avenging of the insult."

Sescnen's trembling was obvious to Labran close beside him, and pity took him now that the moment was upon his helpless kinsman, and vengeance was to be let loose.

"Cousin Leary," he said, and against all custom, moved a little closer to the King. "Cousin, what of our kinsman here, yours and mine, who has no true deep guilt in this?"

Leary looked at him from under the heavy shelter of his

brows, and none could see the expression of his hooded eyes. His voice was dry.

"I leave him to you, cousin," he said. "I leave him to you. Do I not give you land and cattle to be my judge?"

Labran almost smiled. They were past the King, who had chosen in his own indirect way to be merciful. It remained only to deal with Kiann, and if the child were safe, that might not be too difficult. His poor foolish cousin might yet go safely home to his dun.

Leary stretched and sighed in his great chair. His Avenger of Insults should deal easily with this threat from a foreign church. For the moment. He was no fool, and knew of the power of the Church of Rome, and did not deceive himself into thinking that it would not in the end reach its hand into the land of Erin. But this would hold it off at least yet a while. How fortunate this simpleton cousin from the Western Sea should have given him excuse to attack with arms and wipe this fellow Patrick from the land before his feet had steadied on its soil. It was the simplest way, and saved him from thinking of any more subtle methods. He smiled broadly, pleased with himself, and at the end of a long irritable day his household all looked relieved and sagged a little in their chairs, and smiled also to themselves.

The High King waved a hand to dismiss those close about him, and turned contentedly back to his grianin. That fellow Fergus thought he had him cornered, but he still had a move or two in hand. He smiled again as he flopped down onto the colored cushions of his couch and thrust out a foot to the servant to remove his shoes. Almost idly he raised a hand across the chessboard and made a move, lifting his eyes to grin in broad triumph at the flabbergasted face of Fergus.

Labran took the bewildered Sescnen by the arm, and led him out of Caher Crofin.

Chapter Seven

In spite of Labran's anxious urgency, it was four clear days before the chariot wheels and the hoofbeats thundered in the silent dawn, as Kiann led his army of vengeance from the Hill of Tara. Four days allowed to him to summon his men to meet him on his journey of war; the warriors from the fields and hills and the rolling, fertile plains of Meath itself, who stood in the King's service but did not dwell in the great barrack halls of Tara, but in their own homesteads with their families; tilling their fields and tending their cattle until such moments as this, when Kiann sent forth the call to arms, and they gathered under his banner to avenge their King.

Labran went with them—and Sescnen, who seemed during these four days of waiting to have fallen into the grip of age, as he watched the preparations for destruction and death, to be loosed on so many hapless people by his carelessness.

"Can you not simply kill me, who am responsible?" he pleaded to Labran, "and leave alone those who are guilty of no fault." He was thinking of the dun of Dichu, crammed with the innocent who did no more than follow Patrick, many of them his own people, who had gone at the same time as Macha. "Kill only me," he begged. "I alone am at fault."

Labran looked at him sideways, pity and mild contempt in his glance.

"It is not too much to say now, my poor cousin," he said dryly, "that it no longer concerns you at all. You are but one of Fergus's pawns on the chessboard of the King."

Sescnen was not as simple as he thought him. He nodded sadly, and his eyes were on the warriors tramping in steadily along the five roads, gathering to Kiann's bidding in their saffron tunics, with their handstones resting in the hollows of their dark blue shields, and the points of their spears tipped for terror with the blood of adders. Sescnen looked at them, and shook his sad head.

"I know," he said. "I know. It is no longer me. But does it take all these to kill one man?"

Some of them were Chiefs, not long ridden away from the Festival, and Labran knew them as they rode back.

"Losken of the Crooked Teeth. He must have nearly a hundred men."

"Tinna of the Long Arms. Thirty, would you say?"

64

"Kiltan of the Hill."

"Kethen of the Bright Face. Forty men."

They all looked cheerful and gay, laughing as they rode or marched. They were looking forward to a battle. They knew of Dichu and his strength, and the fighting should be good. Life had been too peaceful of late.

"All these," said Sescnen again heavily, watching the bright gathering of the warriors. "All these to kill one man. And I tell you, Patrick will not defend himself. One of these would do, just so long as he has a sword." He could not believe that this monstrous situation had grown out of that spellbound evening in his hall.

"He himself may not resist," answered Labran. "But the man Dichu has given him shelter, and therefore must be destroyed also. And his dun above his head, and from what I have heard of Dichu, he *will* resist. He will not wait and take his death in quietness from The Avenger."

Sescnen took his eyes from the figures plodding up the green slopes of the Hill, and from the golden stretch of sunlit fields beyond them, and the fair country of Meath, and laid his despairing head down into his hands. He remembered the evening two days ago now, when they had left the High King, and Labran had led him through the soft spring darkness in the sputtering torchlight, down the long eastern slope of the Hill to the Raths of the Warriors, and the road that led out toward the fields and dwellings of the soldiers who lived always in the King's service.

At the painted door of the dwelling of the King's Champion, Labran was bidden a warm welcome. He had been there frequently of late, arranging matters for Kiann's coming marriage to his daughter, and the young man stood up from the couch behind his table and came to greet him barefoot; with outstretched, welcoming hands, bidding him be seated beside him and calling to his servants to bring more wine. Kiann of the Crimson Cup, they called him, as well as his more warlike name, for his well-known love of the sharp dark red wine of Gaul, tart and bitter to many of the sweet-tongued Irish.

"Keep your wine, Kiann my friend." Labran lifted a forbidding hand. "We are on the King's business."

Kiann's gaze sharpened and swept over the two men, and beside Labran Sescnen stared sadly at the tall young warrior, and could have wept then and there for his beloved little Macha, that he had so unwittingly destroyed the plans for her young life. She should have had a proper chance to choose for herself, knowing of both, between the teachings of Patrick and life in the house of this noble youth.

Sescnen was not himself a short man, although thin and light, but he felt the size and weight of a young boy beside the warrior who towered above him in the lamplight, easy and ungirt, excused on this informal evening from attendance on the King. His long curling hair fell to the shoulders of his sea-green tunic, so smooth and fair that it was almost white; and gold gleamed warm at his wrists and neck. On the table lay his Champion's Collar, the most coveted award in all the Military Schools, and beside it the wide enameled belt that held his ivory-hilted sword, the heavy tassels of yellow silk falling from it to the rushes on the floor. He was rich and noble and handsome and important, and all these things were in his face. Yet there was there, too, an open, genial kindness that touched Sescnen more with guilt than any of his riches and position.

"The business of the High King?" echoed Kiann, and the open amiable face grew still and watchful. He was like a resting animal that scented danger, and to Sescnen he seemed to grow even larger in his quietness. Even the calm and polished Labran, with all his life of position and authority behind him, found it difficult to begin and carry on his tale, facing the growing coldness of the fair, handsome face.

Kiann turned on Sescnen, and the icy, furious blue eyes

raked him up and down. Behind The Avenger, Sescnen was conscious of bright, cheerful faces; eager warriors with death for their profession and the sword for sport, unconcerned as to the causes, but their eyes lighting at the news of trouble.

"This man, you say?" Kiann's big bare feet took a step toward Sescnen through the rushes. Labran moved between them.

"It is not he who took her, Kiann. He is not the one for your vengeance."

Kiann did not take his eyes from Sescnen.

"I am most fiercely moved to kill this one. He let her go. I am moved strongly to kill him now." The threat was dark and true on his face, and his cold glare was that of The Avenger, no longer the blue, genial gaze of the promised son of Labran. He seemed aware of no one else but Sescnen.

"Kiann, my son!" Labran's voice was clear and cold like a bell, the judge's voice, ringing through the dwelling, and ringing through Kiann's anger, until it pulled his reluctant eyes from Sescnen, and brought his mind back to the man who spoke. "Kiann, my son. Forget him, at least for the moment. His guilt is small. Let us first settle the business of the High King."

Now Kiann was fully aware of him again, and the cold blue eyes flew wide.

"The business of the High King?" His voice was soft and fierce with anger. "Is it only the business of the High King? Is it not my business? Was not Macha, the Little Red One, to be my bride? It is my business, and I will take my sword, the Answerer, and I will find this man from the sea; and I will kill him. And if life return to him seven times, then I will take it seven times, and turn then on those who have sheltered him, and the sword and the brand shall leave them neither life nor lodging."

Labran stood and was silent, knowing that this was how

it would be. He had understood from the start that Kiann would not undertake this with only his loyalty to his King to drive him, as he undertook most of his battles. There was more in it this time for him, for this betrothal to Macha was not as many marriages, arranged between strangers with suitable guarantees of position and cattle, knowing nothing of each other.

This fair mountain of a young man had a long memory of his own; a memory of a small red-haired girl who had pulled his curls and tugged at his bracelets when as a boy he had visited in the dwelling of Labran. He had forgotten her when she went away to fosterage, but when he came to the age to seek a bride, some old memory of affection had crept up and prompted him to go to Labran and ask him if his daughter was of marriageable age. Labran was touched and pleased, hoping for a marriage for his daughter of the same happiness that he had known with Bres, and young Kiann had waited with some secret delight that he would scarcely admit for the return of his small red-haired memory.

Now he was raging with anger, cheated of some fragile happiness before he had even known it; shouting for his captains and his runners with the candles jumping in the violence of his movements, and the spilt wine a crimson stain across the table. He was determined that his disappointment should be avenged with violence. He had no care about the King. This was his revenge. Almost he had forgotten the two men who had brought him the news, until he nearly stumbled over the hapless Sescnen who could not move fast enough to leave his way. He glared at him in blind, blue fury.

"In fetters," he cried. "In the Rath of the Hostages until this thing is done. And if the girl is dead, it will be my sword to loose the red blood from his neck!"

"No, Kiann." Labran planted himself firmly in front of

68

the furious giant. "The girl is my daughter, and remember that I, too, would see justice done, and her stealing avenged."

"She was not stolen," whispered Sescnen hopelessly. "She went." But no one listened to him. He shook his head against the impossible thought of Patrick taking anyone against their will, but Labran went on speaking to the impatient and angry Kiann.

"I will hold him at my side," he assured him. "If we get her back, then surely we can spare him. Kiann!" he said clearly and sharply, as if to remind the young warrior of something he had forgotten. "Kiann—she is my child."

Kiann stopped his angry bustle and stood still, looking down at last at the older man as if he saw him, and thought of what he felt. After a long moment of silence, he made a gesture of submission.

"You are my father," he said, and bent his fair head. He reached out and took Sescnen's limp hand, laying it on Labran's arm.

"He is yours. Guard him well, for if I do not get her, I may yet have need of him."

So it was that the company of warriors set out four days later at the first light of day. On the earthen walls of the Rath of Labran, the thickets of young trees on the sloping ramps were soft with new green, and the long, wet grass was cold about the feet of Bres and her children, who had climbed the steep walls to watch the warriors go.

Bres's heart was as cold as her dew-drenched feet, and she had no thought for the calling cuckoos and the fresh promise of the breaking day. Labran had obediently promised her that Kiann and his men would do all that was needed in the way of fighting. He went only to care for Macha when they found her, and to guard Sescnen as he had promised Kiann. But Bres knew her high-spirited husband, who was no dry-as-dust Druid, for all his cleverness and learning, and she did not trust him to stay quietly in his chariot and remember that the battle was not for him if the smell of blood and dust was in his nostrils, and the war cries ringing in his ears.

Her fears for Labran were drowned in a spasm of fury against her wayward daughter. When the child was safe home, what would she not have to say to her! All the pain and trouble she had caused with her folly! Adze head! Adze head and a new god! The sooner the girl was married the better, and had no time to spare for such nonsense! Adze head! The bright, thundering column had passed from off the Hill, melting into the drifting morning mists that still crept across the plain below, and the last, glinting spear had passed from sight.

Irritably Bres swept her younger children together. Adze head indeed! Kiann would make short work of Adze head!

"Away now and prepare for school," she cried to the little ones. "There is nothing more to see."

Chapter Eight

The warriors camped at last in the tree-scattered fields below the fort of Dichu, coming there in the cool of an evening when mist filled the valleys and crept up in white wreaths to obscure their view of the high hill of the dun, and the small thatched dwellings dotted all over its lower slopes.

Kiann stared at it over the misty distance, and his intent face was puzzled.

71

"There is too much silence," he said at last. "Unless they are altogether dolts, and this man Dichu is not, they must be aware of our coming. There is neither light nor sound, nor any sign of their defense."

Around him, his captains stared with him, combing the distant slope. They walked up and down the dusky fields peering through the soft mist, and the yellow of their tunics was an aching brilliance in the dead light.

"It is odd enough," said one, "that the dun itself is silent, nor does any one come forth to parley." He lifted a hand toward the great bulk of buildings crowning the distant rath. "But are we to believe that every dweller in these homesteads near at hand is either dead or sleeping, at this hour of the evening. There is neither fire nor light in any one of them."

Kiann drew down thoughtful brows, and from a little way apart, Labran watched him, and Sescnen with him, and softly Sescnen spoke of his own idea of the reasons for the silence.

"Dichu is now a man of Patrick's God," he said, "and would therefore have care for all the people who follow Patrick, whether they belong to his tribe or not. All those who have come of late in the footsteps of the priest, and built here around the slopes of his dun—all these will be as precious to him now as if they were his own people. He will have gathered them into the dun, and will protect them with his life."

He spoke with calm and certainty, and in the failing, foggy light, Labran looked at him with curiosity, and wondered how he could be so sure. But before he had time to speak, Kiann had come to his own conclusions.

"He has gathered every soul from these slopes into the rath," he said, beckoning his captains close around him. "And they are many. See all these dwellings over the lower slopes? They are the huts of those who follow this man

72

from the sea, and in addition to his own warriors and his household, the man Dichu has gathered them all inside to defend his dun. The battle will be bloody, my brothers, and desperate, for do not underestimate this Dichu. We will attack in the morning."

The clammy mist lay damp on their faces, and beaded the long limp curls of their hair, but through the moist gloom the captains peered at one another and the grins were broad across their faces, for there was nothing in this world more to their taste than a desperate and bloody battle, with the heads of the beaten dead piled on the battle-field, and the shanachee to take his harp beside the camp-fire when all was done, and sing to them of all their brave and glorious deeds; making a poem of their killing that they could hand down to their children and their children's children, and on forever as long as men were brave. They stamped their chilly feet in the long wet grass and rubbed their hands in pleasure.

"This is good news to my men," cried Kethen, who was called Of the Bright Face. "They grow soft with nothing but the ploughshare in their hands!"

Losken's crooked teeth were white and brilliant in the dying light, a broad grin exposing all their twisted fangs, but Losken said no word.

Tinna of the Long Arms fingered his sword and stared toward the dun.

"It is well," he said. "There will be a pile of heads this time tomorrow rising like the rath itself."

Kiann had not threats or pleasure. This was his business, and his task for the King, but this time it was also a task for himself.

"There is but one head I care about," The Avenger said coldly, "and tomorrow night I will sleep with it beneath my knee. Now we will sleep for tonight, brothers, and gather our strength for the good work of the morning." He took one

last look at the vast, shadowy bulk of Dun-leth-glass, sink-
ing now into the foggy darkness.

"Every man will sleep tonight with his weapons at his
hand. Every weapon at his hand," Kiann ordered. It was
the custom of the men to sleep in camp with one light
weapon by their sides, and the others piled under guard
for easy seizure in the morning. "Tonight," said Kiann
again, "they will sleep with one eye and every weapon.
Were I the man who holds the fort up on that hill, I would
not let this army sleep tonight!"

Sescnen shook his head slowly, quite certain that Dichu
would never attack, by surprise or otherwise, because Patrick would not let him, especially if he had any knowledge as
to why this army was camped below the hill. Not even
when they attacked in the morning would he defend himself, if he knew what was at stake. Even more than at any
time in the previous days, Sescnen's thoughts were numb
and dead, struggling to understand that the morning would
bring the threatened slaughter, and that it was all the out-
come of Patrick's gentle words in his own distant home.
Kiann came up to them in the flame-shot darkness.

"Sleep in what peace you may get, my father," he said
to Labran, looking at Sescnen not at all. Behind him the
misty firelight ringed his head with drifting pink, and they
could not see his face. "Sleep as you may. Tomorrow there
will be blood, but first we will get the little Macha. But
if we do not get her alive and well, there will be red
slaughter such as Erin has never known."

Labran did not answer him, staring through the darkness
in the direction of the dun which they could no longer see,
blinded by the light of their own fires.

"If she is there," he said to himself softly as Kiann moved
away, "I could go and get her, and none would be the
wiser, and there would be no need for slaughter."

Beside him, Sescnen heard his soft voice.

74

"And I could get Benet," he added. Labran turned to him in surprise. In all this business, it had not occurred to him that Sescnen had a hostage up there in the dark dun, just as dear as Macha was to him.

"Yes," he said now. "You could get Benet."

"But it is too late," added Sescnen hopelessly. "Now it is the King's business."

"Yes," answered Labran. "Now it is the King's business." He turned sharply to his cousin in the dim red light. "Do not think, Sescnen," he said firmly, "that I could have done otherwise than take it to the King. I have as little stomach for it now as yourself, for I have small hope that we will get these children out before the fighting. But we of Leary's Household do not have private troubles, or if we do, we may have them in poverty, away from the King. We are Leary's, and so are our smallest affairs."

Sescnen struggled to be reasonable.

"I did not think otherwise, my cousin," he said.

They were talking now almost to keep their spirits up, and against a growing silence as the warriors finished up such food as they had brought and wrapped themselves in their cloaks to sleep, sheltering as much as possible under the trees and bushes from the creeping mists. But for Labran and his elderly cousin there was no sleep, even when their desultory conversation stopped. They sat huddled into their frieze cloaks through the night before a deserted fire, staring hopelessly into its embers, seeing nothing in its glowing heart but pictures of the morning, when they might get Macha back, but there would be no concern for Benet, and death could take a thousand others whose lives were just as precious.

When in the early morning they awoke from fitful dozing, there was nothing left in the clear light of the mist that had wrapped the night. Wearily and in silence they stood up and stretched themselves and straightened their crumpled clothes as the trumpets blared to rouse the men. A moment later Kiann was at their side.

"You have slept, my father," he asked courteously, and Labran answered as levelly as he might that they had. "Now, my father," the young man went on and his face was expressionless, "you will stay in a safe place, well behind the warriors and the fighting, and I will spare a couple of my warriors to protect you and your kinsman."

The words were perfectly smooth and civil, but to the older men their meaning was clear. Despite Bres's fears, they were at the moment no more than hostages, who must not interfere with the business of the King. There was no danger of Labran being allowed to fight. Surprisingly, it was the meek and gentle Sescnen who rebelled.

"It would not be in my mind to run away, young man," he said coldly, facing Kiann and offering him no title of respect. "My son is there in the dun of Dichu, and I would not be likely to forsake him in this hour. That is, if you and your brave warriors leave him in any need of my care."

Kiann was surprised, staring at Sescnen and overlooking the lack of respect. He had not thought the old one himself to be involved in this, but merely guilty of neglect in allowing Macha to be stolen.

"Your son?" he asked, and seemed to see Sescnen for the first time as a person, and not merely as the nameless object of his anger. "Your son? How old is he? And was he stolen also?"

"Macha was not stolen." Sescnen repeated it patiently, yet once more. "She went of her own accord. I only failed in my duty in that I did not stop her." He paused. "My son," he said, "is eleven years. And I gave him to the Roman priest with all my heart."

"You gave him?"

"I gave him. Because I believed in Patrick."

Kiann was no blind, unlettered killer. Nobly bred and of

high intelligence, he was quick to begin to sense that there was more in this than he had at first understood, his mind clouded with anger at the loss of Macha. But now, like Labran, he was in the King's hands and taken up with the King's business, and there was no time left to pause and question what he did. He only stood for a moment looking at Sescnen, his blue eyes resting dark and thoughtful on his face, and then he turned and stared out through the tents flaps at the Hill of Dichu. Around the camp, as the bronze trumpets flared to the lightening sky, men were rising like ghosts from the sodden grass, shaking the sleep from their eyes, and rolling up their cloaks and reaching for their weapons.

"There is no time now for talking," Kiann said briefly, and Labran thought he caught the shadow of regret on the young face. "Remember to do as I have bidden you."

He turned without further words to where his squires waited for him, one with his ax and his round blue shield, the leather handhold ready to his grip, and the heavy silvered belt of the Answerer. The second held his banner, high and bright upon a pole, to be carried over his head. While he buckled on his sword and slid his palm through the grip of his shield, the two older men watched and did not speak, but as he moved away to join his captains, they moved too, aimlessly across the field, pretending not to notice the two armed warriors who closed in behind them.

They ignored the crowding men who pushed and grumbled, mustering to the bright banners, and stood in silence looking across the wakening land toward the Hill of Dichu, on this side a steep, steady slope up to the tree-grown raths that defended its crest, inside the gray teeth of a ring of standing stones. In the fortress at the top there was still an utter stillness and no sign of life, rather as though everybody there was even yet asleep, and oblivious of the enemy at their gates.

"I do not understand," said Labran, and his fair hair was rumpled by the restless fingers he kept dragging through it as he stood to watch. "I do not understand. Will they not defend themselves? Why are they not moving? They must know this army is here."

The same problem was troubling Kiann, where he stood among his captains.

"It is as though we would attack a grave mound," he said uneasily, "with all those we hope to kill already dead."

Like Labran he stood and stared up toward the dun, but in his trained body there was no restlessness. It was this unearthly stillness and silence that made him anxious, not for himself, but for an unease which he could feel behind him, slowly creeping through his men, most of whom were also standing now as he was himself, staring at the dun, with growing expressions of doubt and fear. Kiann knew, without a backward glance that this was so, and knew also that this fear of something they did not understand could sap their will to fight, and lose a battle before ever a sword was drawn. If there were no life in the dun, then life must come from him. He swirled away from his captains, moving swiftly through the men to rouse them and stir them to vitality, crying out his orders for the attack, to take place as soon as he himself had taken up position.

Sluggishly they turned to follow him, their eyes still clinging to the dun, but before he had gone ten paces, Kethen's voice was lifted to follow him.

"My lord Kiann! Someone comes! Someone has left the dun!"

Kiann turned back, and felt the whole mass of men around him move with a long stirring sigh, whether of relief or what he could not guess. No doubt it was relief to them, to see the situation returning to the shape they knew. Someone was coming out from the fort to parley. This was normal and this they understood.

78

"They come," said Losken greedily, and his crooked fangs scraped his lips as he talked. "They come to ask for mercy. Let them seek it elsewhere. We have none to give!"

"It need not be so," Kethen answered. "It may be that they come to make terms for the battle."

Kiann's eyes were more thoughtful, and his hand crept to the Answerer's ivory hilt.

"It may be," he said, watching, "that they will challenge to single combat, to save their dun." He tried to keep the rising hope out of his voice. Never before in all his days had he felt such a creeping distaste for a battle as was growing on him for this one, even though he despised himself for his weakness and stamped on his feelings, lest in the strange way that such things happen, they would spread from himself through his men. He could not shake off this growing feeling that there was nothing here for a King to fight about. Nothing but one child run away, and easily brought back, and another here, it seemed, with all his father's heart. Both might die, and who then would be avenged? Wearily he knew there was more to it than this in the eyes of the King. Leary saw this Roman as a threat to Erin and wanted him destroyed, and the occasion of the stolen girl was merely seized upon as an excuse. It was not for his Avenger to question who might die in bloody battle as he carried out his orders, but Kiann could not free himself of the memory of Sescnen's sad and quiet face as he had told him of his son. The man was only a lesser Chief, but he had some dignity that could not be gainsaid.

Kiann's whole spirit lifted hopefully to see the small figures on the distant hill. Little could be seen of them yet, save that there was one all dressed in white and another in the saffron tunic of a warrior. The third was very small. Kiann fingered the hilt of his sword and rehearsed the formal words with which he would accept for himself

79

the challenge to single combat. In this way, he alone could go out there and fight for his young bride. She would come safely home and the King's honor would be avenged, and that poor quiet creature with Labran could go in peace back to his dun. With his son, if he wanted him.

Behind Kiann, the warriors broke apart protestingly to allow the rush of Sescnen and Labran from their places at the back, followed by their two angry guards who would not be left behind.

"My lord Kiann!" Sescnen could hardly speak in his haste and excitement, lifting an arm in its crumpled sleeve to point up across the fields toward the group and gasping and swallowing to find his voice. "My lord Kiann, it is he! It is Adze head himself! Speak with him my lord, and I promise you all will be well."

Kiann did not even notice that in his answer, he acknowledged his reluctance for the battle.

"There is a warrior with him. It may be a challenge to combat."

"That will be the man Dichu! But that is Patrick! See the light in the disc above his brow!" His arm fell and his voice with it, and his face grew gentle. "And the child with him," he said, "is my son, Benet."

They all looked together at the man advancing down the hill, and even as they watched, the sun reached him and struck a blaze of dazzling gold above his forehead.

"Adze head is come," said Sescnen, and this time Labran did not look impatient.

"Speak with him, my son," he said to Kiann. "There is no honor lost in parley."

Kiann appeared to make up his mind. He turned to them with the firm voice of a commander, and the uncertainty was gone from his face.

"True," he said. "There is no honor lost, and I thank you for your advice. Now Labran, my father, you will come with me, and also your kinsman. Also you, my Kethen of the Bright Face, and you, Tinna, and your squires and banners. The rest of you will wait and watch with all your eyes, and at the very smell of treachery, then you, Losken, will order the attack." He glanced up once more at the open fields crowned by the vast mound of the dun. "I do not forget our open position at the feet of this man," he said. "But I will trust his wand of peace. Dichu is a man of Erin, though we know nothing of the Roman."

Thus he argued with himself, but nevertheless set out firmly over the fields, followed by his bidden men, the green and blue and scarlet of their banners sharp and brilliant in the young light, and their footsteps black in the disturbed dew. At the foot of the hill, Patrick and his companions halted and stood to wait for them to come, and behind them Losken and the warriors watched and waited, and over all the green-gold plain there was silence and a puzzled patience.

Kiann marched fast and steady, so that the older legs of Sescnen had to struggle to keep pace, but as they advanced toward the stream, it was Benet who could not wait at the last moment for the formal greetings proper to the parley, rushing to the very edges of the water, ankle deep among the kingcups, as Kiann's party halted on the other side.

"Greetings, father!" he cried, staggering for his foothold on the sloping bank and laughing, full of happy confidence that with his father and his Father in God come together there could be no danger, in spite of all the warriors. "Greetings, my father! We didn't expect you here."

The tall warrior beside Patrick stepped forward, freeing a hand from the leather leash of the two great wolfhounds to move him back, speaking to him. Benet looked up at him and then moved back to his place and composed himself again, but he could not quench the beaming smile he turned on his father. Sescnen's tired face was crumpled with happiness as he lifted a hand toward the child and smiled back at him, but he did not speak, knowing what was right. He left the forward place and the first words to Kiann, whose squire carried the white wand of parley.

Beside Patrick the other warrior stepped forward, his two huge dogs quiet at his hand, and he faced Kiann across the brown bubbling waters and the yellow flowers of the little stream. Labran, watching, felt a breath of wonder stir in him at the sight of two such men. Dichu was somewhat older than the King's Avenger, a little taller and as dark as Kiann was fair, but both were mighty creatures, perfect in the pride of their youth and strength; the weight of shield and sword and heavy ax as light as children's baubles to their hands; the sun on their long hair and their yellow kilts fluttering to the morning wind. Across the narrow water they stared at each other in hostility and suspicion.

"Who are you?" cried Dichu. The huge dogs moved restlessly at the loudness of his voice, and his squires drew close behind him in the moment of challenge. "Who are you, and where do you come from. If I must fight you, stranger, then tell me the cause of our battle! Who are you, Man of the Bright Hair and what brings you with an army to my gates?"

He was understandably hostile, but his voice too was genuinely puzzled, and the priest beside him looked long at the weary and tousled Sescnen, and the company he kept, and was obviously as puzzled as Dichu himself.

Kiann answered them.

"Not of the Bright Hair," he shouted, "but of the Bright Axe! Kiann of Bright Axe, oh Dichu, Avenger to Leary, High King of all Erin. I am at your gates to seek vengeance for an insult offered to the King!"

Now Dichu and Patrick looked truly astonished, and turned to stare at each other as though asking by all they believed in, what this thing could be about. Benet peered from face to face on first one side and then the other, trying to decide if the conversation should concern him.

"What insult is this?" Dichu cried. "I know of no way in which I have given insult to the King. State your complaint, Champion, and I will answer it, and with my blood if need be!"

"It is not you who have offended the King directly, but the man of strange faith who stands there at your side. And as you have sheltered him, then guilt is also yours."

"Ah," said Patrick. He stood a little more erect and faced across to his accuser, and as he moved the young sun gleamed in the adze blade and flashed a thousand points of brilliance from his crozier. Beyond the stream, Kiann blinked in the bright dazzle of gold, and resisted the strange thought that suddenly the man on the other bank had seemed to grow a little larger.

"If it is I," cried Patrick, and his clear, measured voice reached back through the quiet morning almost to the watching warriors. He planted his crozier firmly on the ground as if to give strength to what he said. "If it is I, then tell me what I have done. I can meet my own charges in the name of my God."

Kiann turned and laid a hand on Labran's arm, drawing him a little forward.

"Labran of the Long Memory is Chief Brehon to the High King of Erin. What touches him touches the King also."

Above the forked brown beard, the mild face of Patrick was utterly bewildered.

"Friend," he said, "I have never seen this man before."

"No, but you have seen his child, sent in legal fosterage to the dun of the Chieftain Sescnen, and stolen by you when you left the dun."

Hopelessly, like an echo, Sescnen said, as he had said at all times. "She was not stolen. She went of her own wish."

No one heard him except Kiann, who looked at him a moment and faltered, as though to hold his position at all he must tell the facts as he thought them, and allow no argument. He turned back across the stream, taking his great ax from the hands of his squire. His feet wide planted in the flowering grass, he took a deep breath and lifted it above his head.

"I charge you," he cried, "for your crime of stealing the daughter of Labran, to defend yourself as best you can from the vengeance of the King; both you, and those who have sheltered you. But first you will deliver up the girl!"

Benet's face was small with anxiety as he listened, and across the small, dancing stream, his eyes were on his father. A couple of times he lifted his desperate face to Patrick, as if he was about to speak, for there was no doubt now that the conversation did concern him, and very closely. The priest's face was a mask of honest bewilderment, and he shook his head as though to clear it, and the light moved back and forth above his brow. Dichu's looks had grown black as thunder, responding at once to the threat of the brandished ax, ready to fight on the spot if need be, without waiting to understand the cause. It was enough that this fair-haired fellow, King's Champion or whoever else he was, should stand here on his land and threaten him for something he had never done. He moved toward his squire as if to exchange the dog leash for his arms, and quietly Patrick moved a step in front of him.

"Peace, Dichu, my friend. In God's name, peace. We have not stayed dark and silent all the night in order to prevent attack, simply that we may lose our tempers in the morning and fight over something we don't understand."

He lifted his voice to Kiann across the stream.

"Now tell me, friend or enemy, whichever you may be, what child is this you speak of?"

"The daughter of Labran, the High King's Brehon."

84

Patrick bent his head, and the gesture was too humble for conscious patience, but Labran felt as if they were rebuked. "This I understand," Patrick went on, and where the others shouted across the stream, his clear voice carried with no effort. "But when or where have I taken her from her parents? The only child I know I took with me from the dun of Sescnen is the boy Benet. And he was given to God with a full heart." He looked over at Sescnen and laid a hand on the boy's head, but Benet did not look in the least blessed by the gesture. With every word of talk, his face was growing more and more unhappy, dark and embarrassed with the certain shadow of guilt.

Benet could keep quiet no longer. With one last glance at his father, he turned to Patrick, his face scarlet up to his springing curls, and his fingers twisting wildly in the tassels of his girdle. His thin treble was like a bird in the silence.

"My father in God," he blurted out. "I know of her. I have caused all this!" He waved a frantic hand at the massed, silent warriors on the plain, and the fringe of people that now crowned the raths of Dichu. "I have caused all this! I alone knew what Macha did, and I didn't tell my father. I know where she is now!"

Chapter Nine

Once again it was the timid Sescnen who took action, while all the others stood by in astonished silence, looking at the frightened boy.

"We must cross the water," he cried. "This cannot be talked out at the top of our lungs with a stream between us." Before the bewildered Kiann had gathered himself to think what was proper to do in this strange situation, Sescnen had skipped nimbly past him and his banners and his squires and his wand of peace. A little farther along the bank, he scrambled down the slope to where a row of big stones gave foothold above the sparkling water. Gathering what position he could, Kiann stalked after him and crossed the stream with his following to the opposite bank, where the small boy tried to hide his face against his father's tunic. Firmly Sescnen stood him away.

"Tell them everything, my son," he said. "You have treated no one fairly."

"I tried," cried Benet, "to treat everyone fairly. I couldn't stop her from going! She wouldn't listen to me! But how could I tell about her and have her stopped? Was I not going to follow Patrick? Had she not the right to follow him just as I?" Unhappily he poured out the whole story of how Macha had told him she would go, standing small and defensive in the ring of tall men who watched him with dark and furious faces, realizing that they had gathered to do battle over nothing. "Had she not the right," he demanded again at the end, "to follow Patrick just as I did?"

"No," said the priest firmly, before anybody else could answer. "No. You had your father's consent. She is too young. How can she learn to follow God if she cannot follow firmly the rules of her father's house?"

Labran looked at him sharply, and the priest looked quietly back.

"I would not snatch your child from you, my friend. Even for my God. Benet was given." His strong, handsome face creased a little almost as if he were embarrassed. "There are many good women who follow me, and gladly allow their daughters to become servants of Christ, and many pious women of their own accord who make me gifts and lay their ornaments on my altar. But I give them back to them, and they are offended that I do so, but only thus can I be sure they follow me for God alone. I preserve myself cautiously that men will not say they follow me for

87

myself." Although his voice was firm and clear, his eyes were diffident and anxious, creased with concern as to how he might appear in the eyes of men, and around him his listeners were silent, more held by his humble honesty than if he had raved and shouted of his God. "But this girl," he went on, "must return to her father's house. There is time for her yet. Benet, my son, where is she now?"

Somehow, reproach had been overlooked, and Benet blinked around in relief that he had got away so easily.

"She is among the women, Father," he answered at once, eagerly. "In the barn."

"Go then, and bring her to us."

Benet forgot he was the follower of the priest, the Chosen Successor of Patrick. He could only understand that, after so many miserable, secretive days, his conscience was clear again, and he could put everything right. On Patrick's word he whipped around from the group of men, and dashed off up the long green slope as fast as he could run, exciting the two wolfhounds with his sudden rush, so that they whined and barked and struggled at their long leash, dragging the squire who held them through the middle of the group. Kiann staggered and was brought almost to the ground, leash and dogs twining around his legs, a tangle of barking and cursing and shouting, until Dichu's firm command brought them panting to his heels. Labran, in his happy moment, waiting for his child, almost laughed aloud to see the gorgeous Kiann, on the business of his King, confused and routed by this muddle of barking dogs and running children. If all goes well today, thought Labran happily, he will soon learn that there is not much that cannot be brought down to nonsense by a houseful of children. Ah, poor Kiann, he thought then, it will not be easy. He has first to settle this business here to his own satisfaction, and what pleases him may not please the King.

The dogs were quiet, and Benet's small figure vanished

into the dun, and in the quiet after the uproar, Kiann was coming to the understanding of his position. Never in all his splendid days as Avenger to the King had he felt so small and useless. He was reared in Military School and on the battlefield, to the pomp and ceremony of challenge and counterchallenge, parley and battle, and the death or glory of single combat. Here he had mustered an army and marched them for days to deal with a prank that lay between a couple of children; nor could he see any guilt in this quiet man before him with the gold gleaming on his forehead; nor in the enormous warrior beside him, speaking easily to his panting dogs who rolled red, loving tongues about his hands. Kiann felt as if were trying to offer battle to the sparkling cobwebs that were drying in the sunshine on the whins. Desperately he strove to remember that the King considered that this priest of Rome was dangerous, and no matter what the excuse had been, it was to kill him that he had been sent.

Patrick looked at him as if he read the heart of his mind, and above the brown beard, his eyes were touched with amusement.

"My poor friend," he said, and Kiann flinched at the understanding in his voice. "There is nothing here for a Champion, is there? There is nothing here to fight." He turned to Labran. "You," he said, "her father. I beg you forgive me, but I knew none of this."

Kiann had not yet found words to answer this quiet man, to restore his dignity and assert himself as the King's Champion. He struggled to find the ferocity that would make further words unnecessary; that would allow him to lift the Answerer here and now and kill this man without more talk, as he had been instructed. That would please his King, and give his restless warriors all the battle they required. But when he looked into the mild, amiable face and met the direct, uncomplicated eyes, his sword hand stayed quiet at his side, and he admitted to himself in amazement and dismay that he could not find the mind to do it.

But Macha touched him more closely than the King.

"There is plenty here for me to fight on," he shouted suddenly, and now his hand dropped to his sword, appalled at the thought that he had come so near to losing her. "She is my betrothed!"

"Ah!" Now Patrick smiled openly. "It was not all then for the King."

"Why do you wait?" Kethen could no longer control his impatience, and whispered urgently behind the Champion. "Why do you wait? They have the girl here! That is enough! Kill first the Roman, as the King wills!"

Kiann listened to the hoarse, fierce whisper, and again he looked at the other group and knew what he should do. It did not need Kethen to prompt him. But against the smiling face of the priest, and the tranquil indifference of Dichu, fondling his great dogs, he knew he could not do it. There was nothing here for battle. The reckoning with Leary might well cost him his head, but he could not bring himself to this act. He drew a hand across his brow and refused to look at the angry face of Kethen, and Tinna at his shoulder. He knew that this moment of decision, even if it did not cost his life, must cost him his position as Champion of the King. Of what use was an Avenger who could no longer kill on order? But he could not do it. He was utterly bewildered, severed suddenly from all the thoughtless, bloody rules that up till now had been the order of his life. Beneath him, his legs felt weak and foolish, as though some great wound had drained away his blood, and in the hot sun he could feel the sweat beading around the edges of his hair. He eased his sticky palm in the leather grip of his shield, and turned away from the exasperated Kethen, breathing deeply to clear his muddled head. Looking upward suddenly to the top of the hill, he saw Macha coming slowly down, hand in hand with Benet.

He had had a great deal of trouble in getting her.

The growing band of women who followed in the way of Patrick had made their living place in the loft of the great barn, which Dichu had given to the Christians for a church. Once safely arrived at the dun of Dichu, Macha had abandoned her disguise and taken her place among the women, telling those few who recognized her that she had been allowed to come, and raising astonished eyebrows when they said they had not noticed her on the journey.

For the first few days, she was ecstatically happy. She understood very little of all she heard, but she was willing to believe and it was enough for her to be within reach of Patrick and within the daily sound of his voice. She felt the time coming close when she would have the courage to go to the priest and ask to be baptised a Christian in the well of Dichu, accepting all she had been taught. She was only afraid that, seeing how young she was, he might ask her of her parents, and to him she could not lie. So she kept always in the crowd and watched him from a distance.

But after a little while, loneliness and homesickness took her like a fever, so that she could no longer hear or listen to anything that was said, drowned in the longing that held her for Sescnen and the family and all the small, happy things of her childhood; for the cool green summer sea and the sliding sand under her feet; the larks shrilling up at morning from the fields below the grianin when she was half awake, and the warm, red fire glowing in the Hall against the winter mists. Her heart ached for her foster sisters, and their parents. And for Benet. Benet was the greatest misery of all, for she saw him every day, the Chosen of Patrick, walking in the footsteps of his master, wherever he might go and sitting at his feet. Benet, always in her sight, while she was under the strict eyes of the older women, was as far from her as the blue unattainable pointed peaks of the distant hills. She was sick with misery and grief, and the Name of God and the Word of God fell into her mind as hollow as the note of Patrick's bell, and no longer had the smallest meaning.

On the misty evening when the news was brought that a vast army of strange warriors was approaching the dun, she was alarmed but obedient, and it did not occur to her for one moment that it had anything to do with her. All those who had followed Patrick and built dwellings on the land below the dun were told to gather into the heart of the fort itself and spend the night in silence and darkness, so that in the gathering fog the enemy could not know in which direction to attack. In this way, action could be held off until the morning, when Dichu and Patrick could go down and speak with these men themselves, and find out why they came.

In the bright dust-laden shafts of sun that pierced the rough timbers of the barn, Macha worked the next morning with her broom, doing her share of the day's tasks and waiting apprehensively, like everybody else, for news of the army below the hill; listening to one of the women who had climbed to the roof beams of the barn and clung there among the startled pigeons, peering down over the walls of the rath at the small, distant figures who talked across the stream. Faithfully, she recounted their every move.

"There is one of them coming back," she called down at last. "Running! He has startled the dogs and there is tumult at the stream! It is the boy Benet!"

"He is running as fast as he can run! Back up into the dun!"

The woman on the beam clutched and craned to try and see closer down beneath her, where Benet had vanished from her sight. By Dichu's order, they were forbidden to open their doors or shutters until they had been told that it was safe to do so.

"He is out of sight." Reluctantly the watcher turned back to the small group still standing by the stream in the soft brilliance of the sun, but there was nothing she could find to say about them.

"They are just standing," she said with disappointment. "But no—I cannot see, but I can hear! Quiet!" she called. "There is someone running along below our wall!"

In the sudden silence all the women looked at each other, and fear grew in many of their faces. Outside there was the thump of more feet running, and voices that called out, and the quick answering treble of a child. Macha's fingers tightened on the rough handle of her broom and her ears grew taut to listen to the padding of the first light pair of feet on the beaten earth around the barn. They stopped only as two fists began to pummel on the great, shuttered doors, and clearly Benet's voice cried hoarsely for Macha.

"Macha! The master says I must have Macha! It is the order of Patrick!"

There were other footsteps then that caught up with him, and urgent grown-up voices who argued with the child. Inside, the round eyes of all the women turned on Macha through the sun-striped shadows, and she looked back at them a little frightened, understanding nothing any more than they did themselves.

"I do not know," she whispered in answer to their unspoken question. "I do not know." The old woman who was in charge of them all frowned portentously and waddled to the door, trailing straw under the hem of her long skirts and with hens scuttering from her path.

"What is it, child?" she called through a knot hole in the wood, torn between her respect for the boy who was the Chosen of Patrick, and the desire to assert her own au-

93

thority. Heavily and anxiously she bent and pressed her great bulk against the door, peering through the hole to look straight and startled into the blue eyes of the boy, who peered from the other side. Benet blinked and drew back.

"I must have Macha, good Mother," he cried again. "Patrick, our Father, bade me bring him Macha, down there by the stream!"

"And the Chief bade me not to open this door," rumbled the old one, knowing that in the end she must give in, but holding to her shreds of dignity by putting off as long as possible the moment of doing so.

"I don't think it matters now about the door," Benet cried. "If you give me Macha, then these warriors will go, I think. Her father waits for her at the stream, too," he added, "and my father!"

"My father!" Inside, Macha dropped her broom and moved toward the door, having her first clear thought as to what all this might be about. But why the mass of warriors? "My father? Has he come to take me home?" she asked the old woman as she reached the door, and did not in truth know how she would feel if he had. She was bemused, knowing that she should cry out here and now that she would never go home with her father, but would follow Patrick as she had planned and promised, and follow his God for the rest of her life. But the loneliness and misery of the last days were like a cloud over her mind and will, and she could bring herself to say nothing. The narrow, rheumy eyes of the old Mother in charge peered at her knowingly from the folds of her fleshy face, and every heave of her bronchitic breath sounded like a reproach.

She turned her own eyes away. "I can but speak with my father," she said weakly, and even as she said it, she felt that she was betraying both herself and Patrick and his God, and all the things she had come to believe in since that first evening in the dun of Sescnen.

94

"I can but speak with him!" Now she almost shouted, defensively, and hearing her voice, Benet cried out again outside the door.

"Macha! It's urgent that you come!"

"You can but speak with him," agreed the old woman sadly, and she moved to lift the wooden bars of the small door set into the big one. "You can but speak with him. May God go with you, child."

Macha acknowledged the farewell, but could not look at her, fiercely denying the finality of it, even to herself. I will only speak with him and then come back, she told herself firmly as she bent to the small door. But when she passed through it, out into the sun, and felt Benet's hard, warm hand reach out for hers again after all the lonely time, she fell absolutely silent. Benet was too excited and preoccupied to notice her distress. He held her hand firmly in his tight, determined grip and led her steadily through the press of people who had rushed from all quarters of the dun, chattering and speculating, but they fell back, and allowed the boy unhindered to lead Macha all along the crest of the hill and out through the great gates; and in and out through the ring of standing stones that dwarfed their young figures and made strange patterns of shadows on the morning grass, and down the steep slope in the end to where Kiann stood at the bottom and watched her come.

It was to the familiar arms of Sescnen that she flew first, forgetting all need for formality, her head on his breast and her face hidden while she struggled under the eyes of all these strangers to calm herself and collect her manners and her dignity. She moved over then to her father, who bent a fierce, uncompromising face to take her kisses on his cheeks, and then she turned to Dichu and to Kiann with gestures of respect, her eyes widening for a startled moment at the strange intentness of the gaze of the fair young man.

"My father!" She began to speak, but her voice was small and lost in the green space, no louder than the larks that shrilled above the hill. Labran was before her.

"My daughter!" With no effort he shouted her down. "You see these warriors?" He waved a furious hand at the gathering on the plain. Macha turned and looked, but they meant nothing, her tawny eyes still dazed and empty. "You see them?" She nodded dumbly and looked at him, not understanding. "They are the warriors of the High King! And this," he moved to lay a hand on Kiann's arm. "This is the King's Avenger, who leads them!" For a long moment she stared up at the young giant above her, and Kiann of the battlefields knew a strange new feeling more disturbing than any he had ever known to take him in the moments of bloodiest danger. Leave her alone, he wanted to cry, looking at the white, puzzled face. Leave her alone! Let the King carve me in quarters if he will, but not another word to her! He moved as if to throw Labran's hand from his arm, but the angry father was before him. "All of them here, my daughter, to avenge the fact that you were stolen by this priest of Rome, and harbored by this man Dichu. Blood and vengeance you have let loose, my foolish daughter!"

Understanding crept slowly into the tense, pale face, and she looked again down over the army on the plain, and back at the tall, still figure of Kiann bearing all his arms, with his squires behind him.

"Oh no," she whispered. Then more loudly. "No," she cried. "No! No one can fight over me for this. I was not taken! I came of my own accord!" Behind her Sescnen held out helpless hands, hearing the echo of his own futile voice. The spirit of her red hair was rising in Macha, and she wheeled on Benet with her white skirts swirling around her ankles. "*You* knew! You knew that I came of my own accord! You knew all the time! Tell them!"

"I have told them."

"Well?" Desperately she swung around the ring of men who towered above her, but it was to Kiann that in the end her eyes came back, screwed against the sun so that she might stare into his face, all formality forgotten. "Well," she cried, and in her excitement she seized the edges of his blue shield and shook it, her pale face flushed now and her eyes sparkling like the peat brown waters of the little stream. "Well, what is there to fight about, my lord Avenger? They have done me no harm. At any time I could have left them. There is no *cause* for battle!"

Kiann stirred as if he had been deep asleep and wrenched his eyes from her face. She loosed her hands from his shield and clasped them, waiting, and when he spoke at last, his voice was slow and heavy.

"There is no cause for battle." Formally he echoed her own words, and there was nothing to show that, if the King's mood were wrong, with these words he could have forfeited his life. Labran looked at him gratefully and moved a little closer.

"It is a good decision," he said. "I will help you with the King." But Kiann did not seem to hear him.

Through all this Patrick and Dichu had watched in silence, but after Kiann had spoken, Macha turned toward the priest, and happiness was wiped from her face again by dark distress.

"My Father in God," she said, and all the fire had left her. Her voice was small and hopeless. "My Father in God, how can I go home?"

"How can you not, my child? It is your place."

"But I came to you. I came to follow you and your God, and I promised I would give Him my life."

"You promised who, my daughter?" asked Patrick gently.

The girl covered her face with her hands, utterly unable to come to terms with this situation which had been thrust on her so suddenly and before so many people. She could not think clearly as to who she was betraying, but she was surely letting someone down to turn and run like this. Dumbly, she let her hands slide from her face and looked straight at the priest.

"Who? I promised only myself, I think." Indeed she did not understand enough yet of this new God to talk to Him as many of the women did, and make promises direct. Nor had she promised anything to Patrick himself.

"Yes," he said now, and his face was kind and quiet. "Yourself. And you are too young yet to make so big a promise. But now you will make one to me."

Macha watched his face and waited, and she felt the turmoil in her grow quiet under the calm, friendly smile. "Learn first, my daughter," he said, "to obey your father in all things, then you will be more ready to learn how to obey God. We will talk of all that again at some better time."

Her eyes widened.

"I will see you again?"

"Surely. I will be with you all again. And may God be with you until then."

He lifted a hand in what Macha had learned to call a blessing, and all the men watched him in a strange silence and did not move, and as he turned away up the hill, her father drew her aside to scold her for all the trouble she had caused, and to pet her in alternate breaths, exclaiming on how tall she had grown and how comely; then to lose his temper again and scold her some more. Dichu came over to Kiann and they spoke together amiably above the rough, thrusting heads of the dogs, and Dichu offered to Kiann and his men the customary great feast to mark their agreement on peace. Kiann thanked him with courteous words, but said his men would not make easy guests, being wild and ugly over losing their chance of a battle, and behind him Kethen showed that this was true, for his bright face was black as thunder and his hand restless on the long hilt of his sword. The two warriors bade each other farewell with much respect, and Kiann turned without another glance at Macha or her father, to make his way back across the stream to his disappointed warriors. Labran and Sescnen came more slowly behind him, the girl between them.

"And now," said Labran a little breathlessly as they climbed up the small bank of the stream, taking a handhold on clumps of yellow iris, and hearing the first angry shouts that rose round Kiann in the distance, "now I am sure, my kinsman, that the next tale that will ring round the hearth fires of Erin will be about the day when the Champion of the High King himself faced the priest of Rome in anger. And of how Patrick laid a spell on him as he stood there, so that he dropped his mighty sword and turned away without a fight."

Sescnen stood still and looked at him. His clothes were still crumpled and awry from his sleepless night, but his thin face had taken back serenity and his smile was the one that Macha had grown up with in the small, happy dun.

"Well yes, my kinsman," he answered Labran amiably. "And was that not just what happened?"

Labran snorted and strode on across the field.

High on the Hill of Dichu, Patrick waited with Benet for the Chieftain to come up with them, leaning on his staff between the tall, gray pillars of the standing stones, looking down across the sunlit fields to the tumult and the mass of roaring anger that was Kiann's disappointed army.

"Think you," said Dichu, and turned with him to watch the milling warriors, "think you that that young man can hold them without their battle? I am not sure that they will not attack in spite of him."

His face was anxious, but Patrick merely looked at him in slight surprise. He gave his crozier to Benet to hold for him, and eased the gold band off his forehead, leaving a harsh

99

red mark in front of his tonsured hair. "The young man?" he said almost absently, glancing down again toward the fields and rubbing his forehead. "Oh yes. That young man will hold them."

Even as they watched, they saw the fair head of Kiann rising above his men, mounted in his chariot with his face toward Tara, and in a moment his white horses leapt into a gallop and he was off, a vanishing patch of color on the green fields. Behind him his men, although slowly and reluctantly, grouped their captains to follow him, and before Patrick and Dichu turned into the great gates of the dun, they were beginning to stream off across the plain.

Down in the fields of the camp, Macha drew back to watch Kiann thunder by, his face set from the most difficult task he had ever undertaken, his fair hair lifting to the speed of his passing and his blue cloak streaming out behind him in the wind.

"Father," she said on a deep breath when the wheels of his chariot had rattled into silence. "I know he is the Avenger of the King, but what is his name?"

Her father looked down at her, prepared to forgive her everything now that he had got her back.

"His name is Kiann," he said. "Kiann of the Bright Axe, Champion of the Collar." He gazed at her with love and pride, delighted to see that in her own fragile, red-haired beauty, she had grown up well matched for Kiann. "I will tell you now, my little daughter, that it is to him that we have promised you in marriage. And do not fear for him for this day's work. The King loves him. All will be well."

He waited for her cries of pleasure and delight, and gazed at her in astonished anger when she burst into a passion of tears. He could not see down into her secret heart where she still cherished the promise she had made, if only to herself, to give her life to Patrick and his God. Homesickness and loneliness had weakened her so that she had broken her promise, and now, as she struggled to remember that she had even made it, he offered her for a husband the most handsome and splendid young warrior she had ever seen.

Sescnen patted her chestnut head.

"She is weary," he said kindly and absently. "She is weary."

His own eyes were turned to the south, beyond the blue points of the mountains, and his mind was on the welcome that would await him at the gates of his dun.

Chapter Ten

The young summer drifted into the high heat of the year, with the wild parsley foaming around the edges of the ripening fields and the voices of the cuckoos failing in the dark woods. Tara lay above the plain like a great long, golden beast, drowsing in the sun while it watched with idle eyes the hazy, pointed cone of the Hill of Slane, standing like a small echo of itself across the checkered land. On the lower slopes of the holy Hill itself, Macha was back among her family.

To Bres and Labran, it was pure delight to have all their daughters around them once again, and in their contentment they did not for the moment press Macha too hard in the matter of her betrothal to Kiann. In all other things she was as happy as her parents in her homecoming, although Finola, who knew her better than her mother, would have found her still and quiet and unlike the bright, tempestuous girl which she had reared, and if ever, in the warm, sunlit silence of the grianin, or across the evening table, the name of Kiann or the name of Patrick were mentioned, or if they asked her of her time in the dun of Dichu, her freckled face would close in stony misery, as if that part of her life must be shut out.

"I don't want to speak of it," she said stubbornly one evening when her father pressed her. "I did wrong to go, and I have said so. Now I am back, can we not forget it. And marriage too. I don't want to marry."

Labran glared at her and looked around to see that no servant had heard the disrespectful speech that was so unlike her.

"My daughter! We are easy with you because you fell under a strange influence, which led you a long way from yourself. Kiann is patient, but it is time you came back to us and faced your life as it is. Forget these dreams of this Roman and all his talk, and turn your mind to your home, and all the things that belong to it. The first of these is honor to your father. Even your Adze blade, or whatever you call him, told you that!"

"Forgive me my father." She dropped her eyes from his angry face. She offered them a clear, loving face, but baffled, they knew that more than half her mind was turned away.

Bres tried to talk to her alone, walking in the scented,

knee-high grass on the round Hill of the Flowers. The bees hummed in the speckled blue of the small, soft-stemmed orchis, and the song of the larks was ceaseless in the high, cloudless sky. Below them, Meath dreamed away into the distance, and Slane was a smudge as blue and tender as the flowers. Over the round crest of the land they sought the tangled hedges for the first blackberries. Or so Bres said, taking in her hand a flat wicker basket, although she knew well that it was barely August, and even on the sun-drenched slopes no berries would be ripe. She wanted to be away alone with Macha, hoping that to talk with her in peace and silence might help the unhappy girl to loose her hold on her secret grief, and so abandon it. For Bres was sure she was unhappy. She saw the shadow that never left her eyes, and knew with sadness and anxiety that through these long summer days that she had been at home the freckled face had grown hollow under the big, tawny eyes, and below the tight sleeves of Macha's gown her wrists were slender and fragile as a bird's.

"Let us rest, Macha, my daughter," she said, when they had rambled a while across the hill, and she had exclaimed with wonder and surprise that the blackberries were still small and green. Her daughter glanced at her as if to say that she knew quite well that she was talking nonsense, but did not have the energy to say so. In silence, she dropped down beside Bres, spreading the wide, brilliant green of her skirts, and staring idly out at the sunlit plain through the soft, waving heads of the tall grasses.

"How secret we are," said Bres comfortably. And indeed they were, hedged by a wall of grass from sight of anyone. She could not have found a time more peaceful or more secret, but even now she did not know how to begin, feeling a spasm of irritated longing for the days when the child was small and she could be told what to do and that would be the end of it. They had hoped so much, she and Labran, from this marriage to Kiann. And now they did not dare to speak of it against the girl's frozen face, but speak of it they must, for even the patient Kiann would not wait forever, and if Macha would not take it easily, then she and Labran would have to be more severe, and she must take it hard. There was no question of altering anything.

"Macha, my small one," she said carefully, and laid a hand on the girl's thin one. "Macha I want to talk with you."

"My mother?" Macha was polite, but she did not look at her mother, her eyes shadowed and wary on the piece of grass she shredded in her other hand.

Bres took it firmly at a leap.

"It is time, daughter, that we discussed your marriage," she said. "Yes, we *must*," she added to the look of wide-eyed alarm the girl turned on her. "Do you not realize," she went on a little irritably, "that your father and I are most patient with you. Most patient! Most parents would arrange this marriage and say nothing of it until your cattle were driven to your husband's home, and it was time for you to follow!" Her voice softened. "But your father and I did not know such a marriage, my daughter, and we would not wish it for you. In Kiann of the Crimson Cup," she used his more homely name, "we thought we had chosen you a husband who would be everything your heart could want. And he asked for you."

Macha lifted the head she had dropped again over the tattered grass, and her eyes were wide and dark as the peat pools in the bog.

"He asked for me?" she breathed, and her mother barely heard the words. "He asked for me?"

Bres looked at her and wondered what chord she had touched. The girl was certainly alive now, a soft flush staining the pale cheeks, eagerly waiting for the answer. Her mother seized the thing that had caught her interest and made much of it.

"But yes. We didn't arrange this match, Macha my own. When Kiann came to the time to seek a wife, he came to your father, and asked if the small red-haired one was yet old enough for marriage."

"That was me?" The girl smiled against her will.

"That was you. He remembered you from when you were small," he said, "fighting him, and tearing the curls from his hair and the bracelets from his wrists."

"I remember him." The brown eyes were dancing now, and Macha's smile broadened to a delighted grin. "I remember pulling his hair! He was very cross."

"Well then, beloved?" Bres looked at her, puzzled. "Well then, what is it that troubles you? What is wrong with the fair Kiann as a husband?"

The smile on Macha's face disappeared as if it had been wiped away, and as her bewildered mother watched, her face crumpled and great tears began to fall, first slowly and then faster, mingling their dark blotches with the fallen petals.

"Macha! Oh Macha my own, tell me what grieves you." It was more than the gentle Bres could bear to see her so distressed. "What is it?"

"Can you not tell me?" she asked gently, when in a while the desperate sobbing eased, and Macha nodded dumbly, as yet unable to bring herself to speak.

"Do you not see, my mother?" she said in a little while, sitting up and wiping her eyes on the hem of her gown. "You have promised me to Kiann." She hesitated and a soft color crept up to flood her cheeks, and for a moment she looked away. Then she looked back full at her mother. "And that pleases me," she said firmly. "What girl would not want to marry Kiann? But I am already promised to someone else."

"To whom?" Her mother looked back at her amazed.

"To the God of Patrick." Her voice shook a little before her mother's expression. "I made my promise to give my life to Him."

"And who did you promise?" Bres asked sharply, even as Patrick had done.

"I promised myself."

Her mother could scarcely hold her patience, all tenderness fled.

"I thought this nonsense was ended when your father brought you home! What matter what you promised yourself at your age! You will do your father's bidding and then your husband's bidding when you are married. All this rubbish of new gods set against a young man like Kiann. It is nonsense to hear a young girl talk so! Nonsense!"

"I know." There was a sad stillness in her voice that made Bres look at her.

"You know?"

"My mother. I remember Kiann, too, when we were small. I have never forgotten, either. And now I have seen him as he is grown—I knew him at once when I saw him on the Hill of Dichu, even if I did not know he was the Champion of the King. Oh, my mother!" She turned and looked full at Bres, and for one startled moment, her mother saw her face as old and wise as her own. "Oh mother, I have *seen* him, and you offer him to me for a husband. And then I have to remember that I have promised myself to the God of Patrick! Oh mother, what can I do!"

"She can do exactly as she is bid," an irritated Labran said, when Bres reported him this conversation as they sat together in the evening peace of the garden, when his day's work was over. He banged down his empty mead cup on the stone seat. "The man himself told her to obey her father! He did not look to me," he added more quietly, "the type of man to lead a child to foolishness. Too steady. He himself told her what to do."

Bres lifted helpless hands and her dark eyes were troubled.

"The girl is young, Labran my husband," she said, "and so full of ideals, and strict with herself about upholding them. Somehow this Roman has caught her up in something stronger than we have understood."

Labran snorted and his fair hair almost bristled. There had been much about this business of his daughter that tried his usual good temper. "Then let her," he said, without sympathy, "catch herself up in preparing for her marriage. There has been enough of this. No better match could be found for her than Kiann."

"But Labran." Bres spoke helplessly, as if she did not expect to be understood. "Labran—Macha *wants* to marry Kiann."

She was not understood. Her husband stared at her as if to decide if he or she had lost their wits, and ran an exasperated hand through the curls on his forehead, standing them up like spikes.

"Then by all the mysteries of the Four Winds," he shouted, "what is the trouble all about?" He stood up to go, the peace of his evening broken. "She is lucky," he added more quietly, "that Kiann was still there to marry, by the time her precious Roman was finished with him, and sent him home to Leary unavenged. And he is lucky to have his head."

Kiann himself thought that he had been lucky. When he looked back on it, he was still amazed and puzzled that the whole business of making his peace with Leary had been so mild and simple. He came thundering back to Tara from the fort of Dichu well ahead of his men, driving himself like a madman, having no patience to offer his charioteer who would not risk his master's neck with such reckless lack of caution. Outside the barrack halls he dragged his reeking horses to a halt, and tossed the leathers to his driver, clinging to the seat of honor. The man drew a whistling breath of sheer relief to be home alive, and stared after him as he strode away immediately in the direction of Caher Crofin, mud-splashed and unwashed and with his hair and beard uncombed, exactly as he had whirled across the fields of Meath.

"He is in haste to meet trouble," the driver said, and climbed down stiffly from the seat of honor, ruefully shaking his head over the state of the overdriven horses.

Kiann crested the sacred Hill with long impatient strides, but as he passed the long stretch of the walls of Micorta, he paused a moment and looked about him. Blackbirds fluted in the tall elms, and beyond the dark gloom of the Grave Mound of the Hostages, the doors of the King were open to the summer night, the light rising to cloud the trees and bushes on the surrounding rath with a haze of insubstantial gold. In the soft, glowing light and the tender evening, it looked a mild and gentle place, and not the dark place of fear into which a man might be walking to meet his death.

Kiann stood a while, unconscious of his weariness and his aching muscles, strained by the long ferocious drive, and thought of what he was about to face. Many, many times, with the hilt of the Answerer warm against his palm, or his Bright Ax whirling around his head, he had come close to death and seen its cold eyes on his face. But if death had indeed taken him at any of those times, he would have known what he died for, fighting for his King.

This time, if he died, and well he might, he would not understand his death. He would die because he had refused to fight, and if his angry King should ask him why, then he could not even tell him. He could only say that he had looked into the steady eyes of the man with the disc above his brow and had known at once that there was nothing over which he had need to fight. Awhile ago, he would have killed every soul on Dichu's hill without a second thought. Nor would it have troubled him when death came to him with the swift cut of a sword or the blunt agony of a club. But now, in the sweet warm evening, with the piercing treble of a blackbird whistling of the summer days to come, he thought of the small, pale face of Macha and the sun on her red hair, and he turned as fiercely and abruptly as if indeed he turned from death itself, and faced toward the meeting with his King.

Leary was sitting in his Hall in his carved chair, and across the table the inevitable Fergus crouched above his chessmen in his endless anguish that his King might beat him, and find him no longer worthy of his high position. The lamps were not yet lit, and the warm dusk on all the faces of the courtiers was mixed with the soft glow of the King's candle and the four wax pillars around the nearest fire.

"Well. My Avenger is returned." Leary's face was expressionless as he turned lazily from the chessboard and stretched his long legs in their tight, cross-gartered trews. Even though he sat at ease, dressed only in his silk tunic, beads of sweat stood along the edges of his curls from the great heat of the Hall. He looked Kiann up and down his mud-stained length, and his eyes were sharp and idle at the same time. "It must have been a mighty battle that sent you home to me like this, my son. And great haste to report it, that would not let you bathe before you came to me."

The rebuke was amiable. The High King had known Kiann since he was a child, and, well satisfied with his service, treated him always with fair words and affection.

Kiann looked back at him and moved to push his tangled hair off his hot forehead. He offered no apology for his condition.

"Oh, my King," he said, clearly and firmly. "There was no battle."

Now Leary was alert. His eyes sharpened, and without appearing to move, it seemed as though his whole big frame gathered itself together into strength and authority.

"There was no battle?" he echoed, and all around the Hall the sensation was signaled from eye to eye, and people shifted quietly closer to hear what was going on. Behind the King, his advisers drew together, and black anger began to gather on Lucru's face. Fergus alone welcomed the distraction to his Royal opponent, and brooded over the table, indifferent to all that was happening, gnawing his nails and trying to see a move ahead.

"There was no battle, my King," Kiann went on, lifting his fair, untidy head and meeting Leary eye to eye, "because I found nothing there to fight over. Two children into mischief, nothing more, and no insult to your Kingly honor."

Leary's thick brows came down over his eyes, and he looked at the young man as if he did not know what he was talking about.

"Children?" he said. "Children? Ah yes. There was a girl involved, or somesuch. But the priest of Rome? You killed him?"

If Kiann breathed more deeply before he gave his answer, he had drawn on all his great courage and self-discipline, and it did not show.

"I found no reason for his death, my King. He had done no wrong, and he was ignorant of the wrong which had been done to Labran, our kinsman. I found no reason for his death," he said again.

There was a long, long silence, and Fergus chewed his finger ends, oblivious, and the tall candle flame wavered in the draught and the wax fell in gouts down its pale sides. Lucru darted to the side of the Royal chair and the only sound was the hissing fury of his voice, while all around the Hall the people held their breaths and waited for the thunder of the King. Leary glared at Kiann through the endless moment, and waved Lucru back into his place, and Kiann held himself straight and quiet and did not look away. At the end of it Leary let out his breath like a great long sigh, as of a man accepting something, and when he spoke his voice was mild and curious.

"You spoke with him, this priest of Rome?"

"I spoke with him, oh King." Kiann remembered the steady eyes across the yellow flowers and the brown torrent of the little stream. "And I could not find the mind to kill him."

"And what did you think of him?"

It was, astonishingly, as if there was no cause for anger in the King; as if he questioned Kiann merely on something of interest to them both. Kiann thought, and tried to answer him as fairly as he could, to try and put into words all the strength and quietness and integrity he had sensed in the white-robed figure on the Hill of Dichu.

"I thought him, my King," he said in the end, "an honest man. And men would listen when he speaks."

Leary appeared to be satisfied with the answer, nodding his head slowly as if he thought much more than he spoke. Labran would have said that this was always so. Lucru darted forward once again, fury clear in his contorted face, but the King waved him away. He lifted his head and looked again at the young warrior.

"I have respect for your opinion, Kiann my son," he said. "Now you look weary and in need of your servants and your bath."

To Kiann, relief was like an explosion in his head, leaving him a little light and thoughtless, so that he spoke the words that were in the forefront of his mind instead of bowing and leaving, as Leary had permitted him.

"But what, my King," he asked, "will you do now about the priest of Rome?"

Leary raised his red brows, and his mouth was touched with a smile.

"What will I do about him?" he echoed. "Well, Kiann my young kinsman, it has brought me small benefit, don't you think, to send my Champion after him. Now I will sit and wait for the priest of Rome to come to me."

"To come to you?" Astonishment robbed Kiann even of courtesy, but the High King let it pass.

"Oh yes, he will come to me. If he is the man you say he is, then this Patrick will have the wisdom to know where his mission must begin." Now his smile broadened into something closely approaching a grin, and he beckoned Kiann closer to his chair. "I am like you, my son," he said softly, for the young man's ear alone. "I do not believe in fighting where nothing will be gained by it. Rome has come, and I know that Rome will stay, in this man's person or another's. But give a wide berth to the Druids, my son, for they will not care for this day's work. However, it may prove to be their turn next to make an effort to defeat him."

He sat back in his chair with a gesture of dismissal, and as Kiann walked dazedly away, he reached out a considering hand across the chessboard, and Fergus groaned and cracked his bony fingers to lose even a pawn.

Chapter Eleven

Decision was postponed for Macha, and for Kiann also. In the early autumn, before Labran had brought himself to force his daughter to anything, news came of a threat to the High King from the Men of the West, who grew wild with power and began to demand freedom from the ultimate authority of Leary. As Champion to the King, it was Kiann's duty to summon all his army as he had summoned them in the early year, and march to the West, setting himself to guard and defend the most dangerous point of threat until peace was once more obtained with the rebellious chieftains.

Kiann came to Labran in the Hall of Judgment in the quiet moment at the end of the day, because he did not want to go to Labran's house, where he might meet Macha, having some deep feeling that, until her mind was settled, he should keep away from her.

"I must leave Tara, my father," he said. "And it may be many moons before I am here again." He faced the older man and despite his warrior's bearing and his gorgeous clothes, and the fair hair that flowed smooth as silk over the glitter of his Champion's Collar, Labran sensed something humble and indecisive in his manner that was never there before. A spasm of anger took him. Was this fine young fellow truly fretting over his wayward daughter! Going thus into a battle, he could lose his life!

"It may well be many moons, Kiann, my son," he answered fiercely. "And on your return, you will be married. This I promise you." He watched, waiting for the pleasure of the definite promise on Kiann's face. "You do her too much honor that you wait so long," he added.

But the young man shook his fair, shining head, almost as fiercely as Labran himself had spoken.

"You will not force her," he said. "She is confused now, but she must come to her choice of her own accord."

Labran was barely able to speak, staring with amazement at the young warrior as if he thought him touched.

"And if she chose the God of Patrick, would you let her go?"

Kiann turned aside a few paces as if he searched for an answer. When he turned back, he still did not look at Labran; his voice was abstracted and his eyes dark and thoughtful.

"It may be she could find a happy answer," he said, "if

she could speak again with this Roman. He said that he would see us all again. But when?"

"You also!" Labran exploded. He had had some measure of patience with the easy conquest of Sescnen because he thought him old and a little simple, but to find that Kiann, of such high intelligence, had also been influenced was more than he could accept.

"I thought he was an honest man," was all Kiann would say, defensively, but now he looked full at Labran and his feet were planted wide and firm, defying anyone to shake him. "But keep her safe, my father, until I am come again to my dwelling. It may be by then she will have forgotten, or have found an answer."

He bent his head with a gesture of respect, and took his leave of Labran, his soft leather shoes scuffing on the earthen floor as he strode away, and the yellow of his swinging kilt soft in the shadows. Labran sat in silence and watched him go, and his mind was full of wonder. He himself had thought no more of the white-robed man with the golden crook than that he had been direct and straightforward and easy to speak with, and sensible about the girl. How could the keen and clever Kiann have seen anything more to make him look back now and wish to have more speech with the man?

"Adze blade," or whatever they called him. He repeated the name in exasperation, and a strange, uneasy thought struck him that Leary had been strangely unwilling to discuss that day's events when his Avenger had failed to avenge, and had not, it seemed, suffered for it. Nor would Kiann talk of what had passed between them, other than to say that the King was not angry. "Leave the future to the future," Leary had said confusingly, when Labran had pressed him, and that was all he would say.

Irritably, Labran eased himself from his chair and gathered his train of servants and advisers for his formal walk home across the Hill after his day's work. Adze blade! It was his intention to go home and tell his daughter firmly that good fortune had given her a little longer to brood on her whims and dreams, but that on the very day that Kiann returned from his present journey, she could make ready for her marriage. There had been enough of this women's prattle!

"Yes," was all she said. "yes, my father." And she bent her red head in dutiful respect. He felt baffled and unable to reach her, and as so often happened these days, he let loose his feelings in irritation, his old easy good temper lost. He shouted at her all he had already said, and she stood there with her bent head and did not answer, until Bres came and laid a hand on his arm, and drew him away to where the bondman waited with his evening mead, and a warm seat beside the fire against the first cool evening mists of autumn.

Thus Macha stayed in her father's home on the Hill of Tara through the late year and the winter. With a mind that did not wish to think of anything else she watched the burning stubble flaming in the cool green dusks across the Plain of Breg as the fields were cleared for the distant spring. She watched the mists creep thicker and thicker over the green hillside as the year went on until for days the spreading plain was closed from sight, and only by their desolate honking did she know of the high geese flying south. The athletic grounds beyond the walls were empty except for the hardy warriors, and the people gathered at their fires with their chessmen and their Storytellers; closing out the nights when frost gathered on the grass and fringed the thatch, freezing the mist in icy sheathing on the trees; and the leather curtains on the dwelling windows grew stiff as boards, beaded with rime along their folds. The dark months crept on for her unbroken, for the Hill of Dichu was the only place in Erin where a Feast of Christmas lit a blaze of glory in the long dead stretches of the winter.

She worked willingly with her mother around the warm dwelling, and walked over the Hill on the stiffened grass; and rode her gray mare on softer days across the plain. She continued her studies with the Druids, although the thin, ill-tempered face of Lucru filled her with distaste, and her father beamed with pleasure at their high praise of her talents. Now, as she had dreamed long ago in the dun of Sescnen, she was in sight of the life of the Royal House, of Leary and his Queen.

She would watch in secret on the nights of the great feasts, when every soul who served Leary on the Hill of Tara would sit down to dine with him, and troops of guests and their attendants, too, until she marveled at the concourse of people that poured into Micorta, blazing through its open doors with light and noise and music.

All these things she saw as she had dreamed so long ago, and she knew the pleasure and excitement in them that she had hoped for, and in her home, too, she showed her parents a calm and untroubled face. Only in her own secret anxiety did she watch the chill daylight stretching ever longer into the darkness of the evenings, filled with the first wild thrilling of the blackbirds, while the brown life of the turning year began to mist the barren plain. Word had come that Kiann's campaign was drawing to an end, and although nothing was said, she knew that soon he would be home again to the pleasure of his grateful King, and the promise of his marriage.

Her parents watched her quiet face, and gladly congratulated themselves that she was forgetting the Roman priest and all he stood for, and they called her to them happily on a day when the whole sky was bright with windwashed light and spring green and tender over all the plain of Meath. Kiann, they told her, with pleasure soft on their faces, was to be back in his dwelling on the Sacred Hill, with all the other Nobles and Chieftains and Kings, in time for the great Spring Festival of Tara.

Up in the North, in the Kingdom of Ulidia, the people of Erin were gathering in ever-increasing numbers to the Hill of Dichu, to listen to the teaching of Patrick, and his name and word of the wonders which he taught were spreading slowly through the land. Through the long months of winter he moved about the countryside, bringing with him the teaching of his faith, and here and there smaller churches were set up within his reach, and a college for the teaching of Irish priests, and the foundations were established of the first monks and nuns of Erin, according to the pattern of Rome. But Patrick fretted because his work was limited. Lest he and his defenseless followers be attacked and killed, it was dangerous for him to move out of reach of the protection of Dichu, but in these early months he laid down the pattern of his work.

Gradually he was gathering about him a Household of dignity suited to his Bishopric, although he himself remained conscious always of his blunt ways, and humble in all things. He began the training of a company of followers of standing and importance, sons of Chieftains and of Kings, raising them in his way of thought so that, when death would claim him from this adopted land, there would be those left behind him who would be well capable of ruling their Christian Erin, but the young Benet he trained at his own side as his Successor.

Wherever he went, he always sought out first the Chieftain. If he could not move him with his preaching, then he found often that he could move the wife and children, so gaining the favor of the men, and safety from attack within his district. He was a realist, as was his Church, and where the Word of God fell on empty ears and hearts, he bought his safety generously with cattle, for the Irish had no coinage and no use for Roman gold. With purchased time, and freedom from attack, he could gain the common people, who were often then followed by their reluctant Chiefs. In the Kingdom of Ulidia, Christianity had taken a firm hold, and belief was warm and strong, but even with success, Patrick was restless. The Word of God was traveling too slowly, and in too small a space of Erin. As the Spring, which brought such fear to Macha, came creeping over the soft undulating country of Ulidia, Dichu noticed that his face was sober and preoccupied, and that he stood often in these wild, windy days on the highest rath walls, looking thoughtfully southward over the awakening land.

The Chieftain came to him one day as he sat there, striding up to him along the steep slope of the rath, with his two great dogs pulling at their leash. The priest was sitting alone, simple in his white woolen robes with no golden adze to hold his hair, which lifted and fluttered behind his tonsure in the rough, salty wind from the sea.

"Ah, my friend." Patrick smiled and moved a little way along the trunk of the great elm on which he sat. It had come toppling in the gales of winter and now lay stripped of all its branches, waiting to be taken to the sawmill. "Come sit with me. If these gentle creatures will allow you!"

Dichu smiled too and spoke firmly to his dogs, who sat unwillingly on the ground, finding the command difficult in their eager affection for the man on the fallen tree. They sat, but they strained and panted with long, pink, dangling tongues, trying to reach and caress the gentle hands that touched their heads. They were well trained and did not move.

"They are splendid, Dichu, and a credit to your training. When I go from here, I beg a pair of them from you for a parting gift. I have missed my dogs in the long, studious years. When I was a youth with my master's sheep on the

Hill of Slemish, they were my pleasure and my company."

Dichu sat down beside him, his long legs doubled up and his hands dangling over his knees. His face was easy and content as he turned to Patrick.

"With all my heart, Father," he said, "you shall have the pick of the pack. But that will not be for many a long moon."

He spoke tranquilly, believing what he said.

Patrick watched him with affection, and did not answer for a while.

"I will be going very soon, Dichu," he said then, mildly, and the man turned on him in grief and consternation.

"Oh no, my Father. Why would you go so soon?"

"So soon?" Patrick smiled a little. "I have work to do, Dichu, my friend. Do you think it is only the lands of your Tribe that need the Word of God? I have taken the safety and hospitality of your dun long enough. I must go forth on my task, through all the land of Erin. I must be about the work of my faithful God, for whom I am ambassador in this land."

"But you have done much work here! See all you have done in the country near at hand! And the people flock from near and far to my barn to hear the Mass and listen to you preach!"

"Ulidia is small, Dichu. I thank you for your goodness and your love, but I must go."

Dichu looked at him for a long moment, his strong dark face crumpled with anxiety, and then burst out with the real fear which lay at the back of his words. In his heart, he knew that, to a man like Patrick, Ulidia was nothing. He must conquer all the land.

"But if you go to a strange country where you are not known," he cried, "how can I protect you?" The man beside him was so mild and humble, so utterly unwarlike, that he could foresee his easy death at the hands of some violent tribe, who would strike first at the stranger and only think to listen afterward. He would never care for himself. "In my lands you are safe," he pleaded.

Patrick shook his head.

"Then I go with you, wherever you may go. I will raise an army to follow you and protect you."

The priest smiled gently and laid a hand on his arm.

"Dichu, my good defender, I know you would give your life for me. And I thank you, but I thank Him too who has strengthened me in all things. I cannot bring the teaching of a God of love through Erin at the point of anybody's sword. I must go, my friend, with no one but my own Household, and such of my following as may be willing to walk with me in peace."

Patrick stood up, and the warrior's face was heavy with sadness. He had grown deeply to love this mild, diffident, humorous man who could yet be so strong and utterly determined in his faith and in the work he had come to this land to do on behalf of his God. Dichu sighed. Knowing him, he knew there could be no real argument about his going. Patrick would have decided before he ever spoke.

"It is time," the priest said now, and the note of his voice was absent, as if he were looking forward to the derision and opposition he would meet, and the battles he must win. "It is time I moved forth to travel this green land." He paused a moment and then went on. "And let those who will, laugh and scorn," he said. "I shall not be silent. Nor shall I hide the signs and wonders which the Lord has shown to me so many years before they came to pass; as He knows everything, even before the times of the world." Dichu was silent, and his heart ached for him. He was always so wounded by criticism, and by those who mocked his stories of the revelations of his God, although, he always faced his mockers with a steadfast quiet.

"And where will you go first, my Father?" he asked dully,

almost without interest. It would be enough that he was gone. The man beside him paused before he answered, and Dichu looked up at some new firmness in his silence. He had the feeling that he braced himself for something.

"I am going to Tara," Patrick said quietly.

The warrior's eyes flew open.

"To Tara!" he echoed, and his voice was horrified. As well to walk now into the sea and drown himself, as go to Tara! "What chance will you have there of life?" he cried. "Leave the King himself aside, the Druids of Tara are the most fearsome men in all of Erin! They will be heart set on your destruction. In faith, Father, you know my own Druids would slit your throat if I took my eyes off them for one long moment! You have destroyed their power here, and the prophecies tell that you will destroy it all over the land. The Druids of the Sacred Hill of Tara will not take that without a fight! Oh, my Father, can you not go somewhere else!"

Dichu stared at him in anguish, looking at his certain death, but Patrick answered him with composure.

"Friend Dichu, my mission has been most successful within the confines of your power. Can you tell me why?"

Dichu lifted helpless hands, and failed to find words for all he would say. He was only a simple warrior, and could not find the phrases for all he thought about this priest.

"I thank you for all the things you have not said." Patrick's voice was a little dry, and a smile twitched at the corner of his mouth. "But it is far from due to me alone. I have preached in your country so successfully because of your protection. Oh, it is true, and most important." He waved aside Dichu's protest. "I have not had to waste my time in raising an army to fight for me, and in fighting first and preaching afterward. Your protection has given me peace to preach."

Dichu was silent, knowing in his heart that this was true.

"Now," Patrick went on after a moment, "I have to seek the same protection from the High King, so that I may have peace to preach in every corner of the land of Erin. Nothing less will do."

"But the Druids!"

The priest's voice was calm. "I must take the Druids as I take all other obstacles in the way of the God I serve. I know they are my strongest and most dangerous enemies. Leary brandished a sword at me in the shape of that fine young man and all his warriors, but the gesture was half-hearted. It is with Lucru and Lucran and their minions that I must wrestle."

The strong face of Dichu was creased with doubt.

"The High King is no weakling," he said. "Do not pass him too lightly."

"Dichu, my son, the Church of Rome is no weakling either, nor does it send its sons into strange lands in ignorance of the troubles they will meet, or the battles they will have to fight. You bid me not to think too lightly of Leary's strength. Well, I bid you not to think too lightly of his intelligence." He went on as Dichu stared at him without comprehension. "I did not come here, my friend, without knowing well of Leary, and all he can mean to me. We have our ways of finding out all the things we would know. And Leary is a brave and clever man—too clever to be unnecessarily brave where it will bring him nothing. I think that he is not at all unwilling for the land of Erin to follow Rome like all the rest of the Empire, but he must answer to his own people. Leary will give me the protection that I need, in the end, but first he will make me fight for it, lest his people think he gives it too easily."

Dichu's mouth was almost open, his slower mind ranging over all this. Some of it he did not even understand.

"How will you fight them?" he asked in the end, coming back to that which he understood.

"You are a great warrior, Dichu," Patrick answered. "Great enough to know that the only way to fight an enemy is with his own weapons. Useless to oppose with a sword the man who whirls a club, and a dagger is no use against a spear. Am I not right?"

Dichu nodded, on his own ground, and then came to understanding of what Patrick meant.

"But their weapon is magic," he said. "You have no magic."

Patrick's face was mild and easy as he lifted it to the spring sun, the dogs heavy on his feet.

"True," he said. "True. I have no magic. I can only go and face them in the name of God, and see what weapons they face me with. Then I shall take what God may put into my hand."

Chapter Twelve

On the sacred Hill the Men of Erin were gathered for the great Festival of Spring. For long days past they had been winding their way through strange, unseasonable, chilly weather toward Tara; along the five roads from the corners of the land, marking the green, cold plain with moving trails of color. The Kings had come, and with them their sons, the Princes, and also their Queens and their daughters. The Lesser Kings had ridden in, and the Chieftains

126

of all ranks, and every brilliant bright-clad Noble was followed by his train of servants and his Poets and his Soothsayers; his Pipers and his Fluteplayers and his Chessplayers; his Deerstalkers and Wrestlers and Champions and Jesters, so that no man could say that another of his rank traveled with a better Household than he did himself.

On the last day before the Christian Easter, a hush fell over the busy, crowded Hill. This was the day given over to the ceremonies of the Druids, to prayers and incantations to the Elements they worshiped. In their striped ungainly robes, with the hair crested on their cold shaven heads, they looked in desperate anxiety at the weather that was already betraying them in icy unseasonable cold, with black clouds gathered like a threat above their Hill as they frantically offered libations for the prosperity of the crops that lay already blanched and withering in the bitter fields.

In the green gathering dusk of the cold spring evening, they reached the ceremony of the dousing of the hearth fire of the High King. Following the blackening of his hearth on this sacred evening of the young year, it was the law that every fire in Erin must be put out until cold and darkness covered the whole land. No fire might be rekindled under penalty of death until the beacon from the Hill of Tara proclaimed across the darkened country that the fire of the High King was blazing once again on his rekindled hearth, and the message of new life in the awakening year spread from fire to fire across the high ground of the whole Kingdom.

Lucru and Lucran led their procession into the great Hall of Micorta, where the tables were cleared from the floor, and the vast long spaces of the Hall left empty, so that the hundreds and hundreds of the King's guests might crowd in to see the ceremony for which they had traveled so far. The tall King's candle before Leary blazed in the new darkness like a monstrous star, and the whole long, shadowed

Hall was filled with the wailing of the stamping, circling Druids, and the thin plucking of their harp strings. The tight-packed crowd stood pressed in silence against their neighbors, awed and troubled by the mystery and strangeness of the hour, as the fires died along the length of Micorta, and the pale flames of the candles faded and grew small against the enormous spaces of darkness.

Macha had been brought by her parents to see the ceremony for the first time. Labran had to leave her and her mother to stand in his official place behind his King, but he had entrusted them to the care of Olbran, a member of his Household, and they stood close together at the very edges of the crowd, where Macha could see clearly everything that was going on. The girl did not, could not, take any interest. She watched in cold and lonely disbelief all the antics and incantations and the strange ceremonies of the men in the striped robes, and it seemed to her as dead and empty as the blackened hearths. She could only remember with an ache of sadness another Hall a year ago in this self-same season with the true softness of Spring, with nothing but a tired voice beside a dying fire, telling, in the silence, of God.

Irritably she turned her head away with a sharp gesture from the shaven, crested heads, and her eyes fell on the group of Nobles who stood in custom close around the King. In the darkness, the golden light of the huge candle fell on Kiann's face, leaving the long fall of his fair hair hidden in the shadows. He was so tall that the flame of the candle was little above his cheek, and in the clear, soft light, Macha saw his face to be lit with a puzzlement and distaste as plain and unhappy as her own. Before she had time to think on this, the Keeper of Micorta's Door came plunging suddenly down the long Hall, indifferent to flung curses and half-drawn swords and the small, shrill, protesting cries of the roughly treated ladies.

Everybody watched him with wide, astonished eyes, but in the open space in the middle of the crowd the Druids still chanted away, unnoticing and undisturbed. He rushed in his rough and anxious progress to the edge of this open space around the central hearth, held for the celebrants, and here he paused to stare wildly around him with a face pale with astonishment and fear, trying to decide whom he should speak with in this unheard-of moment. In desperate anxiety, he banged his fists together and then made up his mind.

From all the mighty Hall a great astonished gasp lifted to the painted roof beams as he plunged into the middle of the wailing Druids. By the light of the tall candle, Macha saw the High King's astonishment, and then saw his face grow black with anger and death come into his eyes. The warriors on duty leapt after the Keeper and among the flabbergasted Druids the thin, sad music faltered to a stop. Lucru's voice wavered into foolishness as his angry eyes rolled at the intruder, and Macha, who hated him, could not keep back her delighted grin.

But Lucru had heard what the frantic Doorkeeper was shouting at him and even as the warriors closed in and his own singing faltered to a stop, he glared at the man with fear and amazement and then gray fury chasing one after another across his thin face. A moment he remained still, as if he could not believe what he had heard, then with one gesture he abandoned his disordered ceremony, gathering up his striped robes and almost running in his haste to reach the King.

In the pale glow of candlelight, Leary listened to the gabbling Druid and his face remained impassive. Only his eyes grew sharp and firm on Lucru's face as he spoke, and then lifted just once to look over the heads of his crowded people as if he stared thoughtfully out through the walls of Micorta to something unseen which lay in the darkening evening beyond them. Nor did he answer Lucru, but reached out and seized his Chain of Silence, clashing the golden bells in his huge hand until quiet spread once more through the Hall and his puzzled people looked at him in silence and waited for him to tell them what was wrong.

He told them nothing, but when they were quiet he glared around at them from under his red brows in a fury that they should raise such uproar in his presence, and then strode in silence out of the Hall, through the pressed back ranks of his subdued and gaping subjects. Behind his back the uproar broke out again and the servants struggled with the closed doors, but so great was the crush that only four out of the fourteen could be opened to allow the mass of astonished people to pour out into the cold dusk, struggling to be the first to see what had alarmed their King.

"What is wrong, mother? Olbran, what is it?"

Macha did not like the struggling mass of people, all striving to get through the doors at once and see whatever might be seen, so that rank and dignity and order were forgotten, and Chieftain elbowed King, and First Grade Nobles were tripped up by shouting Charioteers.

Olbran, the Steward of Labran's Household, had his arms around Macha and her mother, trying to protect them from the worst of the crush.

"Please, Olbran," gasped Macha. "Please get us out!"

There was a terrible silence now in the struggling crowd, determined only on one thing, and being small, Macha was lost down in an even thicker and more airless darkness. Olbran struggled to get them even up against a wall, where he might hold them until the worst was over, but their position of privilege which Labran had so carefully arranged had left them in the very middle of the Hall, caught up by the worst of the pushing torrent, thrust back and forward over the dead hearth itself in a sickening smell of ashes and hot, trampled wax.

Macha began to feel the darkness creeping from the inside of her head, as well as pressing from the outside. Breath was thick and difficult and her legs felt weak and hopeless as she sagged heavily against Olbran. Dimly, as she went down into a roaring darkness, she felt a strong commotion in the crowd, and heard a voice somewhere beside her in the darkness say, "You care for the mother." Through the surging dark mist that wrapped her, she wondered almost idly where she had heard the voice before, and marveled vaguely at Olbran's surprising strength as she felt herself swept up in a pair of arms as though she were a feather.

"Way for the King's Champion! Way for the Avenger!" She heard voices shouting around her, but now they were no more than faint, shooting lights in the dark depths in which she drowned, and of no account to her.

After a while the darkness began to slide away, and her whirling head slowed down and steadied. She felt herself out in the open, with the bitter wind of this strange Spring evening on her face, and gratefully she drew great gulps of it to clear her mind. Slowly the scene around her settled, and she was able to look about her and see the last of the people pouring more easily now out of Micorta, where they had got more of the big doors open. They joined the gigantic crowd, with Leary at its center, which stood in babbling amazement all along the whole ridge of Tara, like a gesticulating fringe against the cold dusky sky. She realized then that it was Kiann who held her in his arms, and she forgot to be astonished by this, staring up at his disheveled hair, and the blue cloak torn from its shoulder brooch, and a long woman's scratch red and angry along his arm. Then she looked in his face, and for a long quiet moment in all the uproar they stared at each other until Macha dropped her eyes and stirred in his arms. At once he put her down.

"I thank you," she said faintly, and made the effort to

stand firmly and with dignity on her unsteady legs, smoothing back her tousled hair, but in the middle of the movement her hands grew still and fell back to her sides, as she realized at last what it was that the High King and his outraged Druids and all his bewildered people were still staring at.

"Oh!" she cried after a moment. "Oh!" Her hands flew to her mouth and her whole pale, frightened face blazed suddenly with wonder and delight. "Oh, Kiann," she cried, and she did not even notice that she had spoken to him and used his name. "Oh, Kiann!"

"Yes," said Kiann above her head, and she could feel his hands warm and firm on her shoulders. "Yes. He said that he would see us both again."

Side by side in the cold, unseasonable evening, they stood on the heights of Tara with all the hundreds who had gathered for the pagan Festival of Spring, and across the Plain of Breg they watched a small fire blazing on the Hill of Slane, scarlet through the green, bitter dusk, a challenge and a sacrilege to the cold, unkindled embers of the High King's hearth.

When Macha turned again a few minutes later, she found Kiann vanished, and her distressed and shaken mother by her side with Olbran.

Patrick had come to the Hill of Slane in the early hours of the cold afternoon, when the Druids were still piping and processing around the distant shape of Tara. He had come to his battle with them as he had told Dichu that he would, unarmed himself, and followed by no warriors. Only his Household was with him, and a few of his most faithful, and also the boy Benet, whose young, fair face looked pinched and weary in the icy cold of the strange brilliant day.

There was no shelter on the Hill of Slane, nothing but the

dark and silent thickets of oak and massive yew, and at the very top, the green, forsaken ramps and ditches of the Gravemound of the Men of Fecc, long dead already in this ancient country when Christ was not yet living. Patrick himself looked exhausted at the end of his bitter journey, and gathered his cloak around him against the wind that drove great tattered fragments of inky cloud across a sky as cold and clear as Leary's crystal window. Several of his devoted Household came to him, and protested that it was impossible for him to stay in such a place.

"It is too cold, in this unseasonable weather. There is not a roof under which to lay your head, or a wall to shelter you from the wind."

"Is there any reason that it must be here, my Father? Can we not find somewhere we can better care for you?"

So said Mochta his Priest, and Coemen, his Chamberlain, and they looked distressed and unhappy. For what was the use now in having a Household suited to a Bishop, if there was no house to keep, and the Bishop cared not for himself?

Manach his Firewood Man shivered, and crossed himself carefully and reminded himself that he was a Christian, even if a very new one, and that he had nothing to fear from the dark, unchristian yews or the poor restless spirits of the long dead Men of Fecc.

"But I think, my Father," he added his objection hopefully to the others, "I think there is not much dry wood around here. Perhaps it would be wiser to do as the good Mochta and Coemen say, and go somewhere more suitable to your station."

Benet looked from one man to the other and a smile warmed his chilled face. He blew on his blue, frozen fingers and waited in silence for the will of Patrick, which was to him with peace and contentment in all things the Will of God. *Benignus*, they were beginning to call him. The

Blessed One. Now, as on many another time, they drew peace themselves from his sweet, unreasoning contentment in everything that might befall.

Patrick watched them all.

"This is the place," he said then. "This alone is the place, and do not fear for the night, my brothers. Our good and generous God will give us all the protection we may need."

As they began on the setting up of some kind of rude camp to house them all for the coming night, he left them and moved off across the hill. Benet turned at once to follow him, never ceasing in his song, jumping from tussock to tussock of the reedy grass with his long thin legs red with cold, and his outgrown cloak flapping in the wind behind him. He halted and grew silent where Patrick himself had stopped on the flank of the hill, which faced across a small plain to a long ridge of land some distance off across the wind-driven country.

"Tara," he said at last.

"Tara," echoed Patrick beside him, and did not take his eyes from the place where he knew that he must surely fight the greatest battle he would fight in Erin, even if there was no sword unsheathed, and no javelin flung. He blinked against the wind which stung the blinding tears from his weary eyes.

The wind. He could not help feeling that there was importance in the wind. O, my God, strengthen me, and help me in every way to lead them to the truth. He prayed desperately, remembering what he had said to Dichu, that he could only wait in this battle to see what weapons were used against him, and then turn and take the one that God put into his own hand. Now he could not lose this feeling that he must take special and careful heed of this unseasonable bitter cold. Seven long years of tending sheep on the northern hills had left him with little to learn about the ways of the weather. He could read the colors of the sky and the shapes and movements of the clouds and the sudden veerings of the wind just as clearly as the more learned monks could read their colored parchments in his far monastery in the warm southern sea. He could smell and sense the coming changes in the still untroubled air, before other men were yet aware of anything, and now all his instincts warned him of strange and violent weather, even more severe and out-of-season than the clear bitterness which already blanched the plain. He lifted his head a moment where he sat, and sniffed the air.

"There will possibly be snow, Benet, my son. There will certainly be a wild and dreadful storm."

He was obsessed with his feeling about the weather, coming to the conclusion that he was so much aware that his battle here at Tara would be with the Druids, that he had almost begun to think in their terms of the Elements.

So he sat there with his eyes on Tara, praying that his God would show him what to do, and lifting his head only to watch the signs he knew so well, above him in the bitter sky. As always, Benet sat at his feet, and was of one mind with him. The cold, green dusk of the uncanny evening began to spread its shadows over the Plain of Breg; the woods grew dark and the dense yews black as night, and the long, populous Hill of Tara turned to a shapeless shadow against the western sky. The priest watched it and never ceased in his prayers, and observed the unaccustomed darkness of the dead fires fall over the Hill that would normally be leaping with a hundred flames. When total darkness wrapped it he stood up, but as he turned to speak to the boy beside him his eye was caught by a bank of cloud, low down in the still-brilliant eastern sky, spreading over the clear evening like a dark, creeping stain. He paused and looked long at it, carefully noting it and what it might mean. Then he turned again to Benet.

"In God's name, son, the first weapon is to hand! Quickly!

Go and get me Manach, and bid him bring me all the wood he has collected, to build me a fire. We will build it here on this high rampart, where they cannot fail to see it from the Hill of Tara. And kindle me a torch!"

Stiff with his hours of sitting, the boy spread his fingers and stamped his feet automatically against the cold, but his face was astonished and his mouth open as he looked at his master.

"But my Father! You know it is the Festival of Spring! You can see that the Fires of the High King are out, and none may kindle a fire in Erin until the beacon of the new season lights on Tara! That is why the men of the Household wanted you in better shelter."

They stood together, the priest and the boy, and looked toward the dark Hill. Both of them stood pinched and weary with the cold, but where Benet's face was astonished and uncertain, breaking his customary peace, Patrick's held the relief of one who has waited in long patience for the flare of trumpets and now goes joyfully into the battle.

"Benet," he said, "it is true that tonight no pagan fire may be kindled in the land until the King shall raise his beacon. But you and I, with the help of our loving and generous God, will light the first Pascal fire of Christ. Now quickly, get Manach and the wood."

As Benet fled to do his bidding, he turned around once more to stare with thoughtful eyes at the black stain of cloud along the low distant sky.

Chapter Thirteen

Over on crowded Tara, the Druids were recovering from
their first fury of surprise. Like Kiann and Macha, Lucran
and Lucru were in no doubt as to whose hand had kindled
the fire that blazed sacrilegiously into the dusk over on the
Hill of Slane. On either side of Leary they almost danced
with rage and indignation at the challenge made so fierce
and public.

"It is the Roman! No one else would dare to do this thing!"

Lucru rolled his eyes to heaven and threw out his arms in a gesture of prophecy.

"It is the Roman, oh my King, and unless this fire which you see be quenched this same night, it will never be quenched, and the kindler thereof will overcome us all and seduce all the folk of your realm."

Leary turned and looked at him calmly, the only one of all the seething, wondering multitude who seemed neither to be surprised nor particularly upset by the sight of the red glow across the plain. Indeed Labran, who was close beside him when they first came out, had surprised a slight smile on the High King's face, and an expression very close to admiration, as if in battle he had found an adversary he thought worthy of his own mettle.

"And how would you advise me, Lucru my man of magic," he said. "How would you advise me to quench it?"

"Go now, go now," the Druid cried, beating his hands together in alarm at the tepid reactions of his King. "Go now, oh King, and answer this challenge at once! Bring the Roman to account that he dares thus to offer sacrilege to the sacred customs of our land! Face him, oh Leary, with your wrath and might, and drive him once and for all from this land, or kill him else beside his unholy fire!"

Even if he had failed to rouse anxiety in the King, Lucru had succeeded in whipping himself into a frenzy. He staggered a little as his voice screeched upward on the last words, and his face below his shaven head had taken on a strange blue pallor in the fading light. Small flecks of foam gathered at the corners of his mouth, and his knees sagged as if he was totally exhausted; too exhausted to care much for his victory when Leary answered him.

"Order out the chariots," he said. "We will do as my Magician says, and answer this dangerous man here and now. Lucru, Lucran, you are the generals of this battle. It will not be one for swords, if all I have heard of this Roman be true. Bring your followers and all your powers! I will take only my Household, and Kiann my Champion, you at my side. Bring out the chariots and we will go at once across the plain before darkness falls."

Beside him, Lucru did not appear to hear. He seemed shrunken into his robes, and he was shivering suddenly as if only at this moment had he felt the bitter wind, and the same cold pallor darkened around his mouth. The messengers fled to the stables with the King's command, excitement winging their heels, and the wide green dusk still held the sky when a train of nine chariots rumbled and thundered down the flank of the Hill which led to the Plain of Breg.

In the front one rode Leary, and beside him Lucru, huddled in his cloak. His eyes were vague and filmy, and for once indifferent to the weather, so that he paid no heed to the great mass of black cloud that was creeping slowly and steadily toward the Hill of Slane, spreading wide across the whole sky, and filling the cold air with the threatening rumble of thunder.

On Tara, the vast crowd still stood and watched, huddled in their cloaks but oblivious to the weather, even though there was now nothing left to watch except the small, steady point of light on the far hill. Macha was no longer watching this. Her eyes strained after the chariot train until they were swallowed up in the tree shadows of the plain, and she had no thought for anything except the fair head of Kiann, rising above all the others in the chariot following the King. For the first time, consciously, she prayed directly to her new God, and begged him to bring the young warrior back safely to Tara. She did not even remember to pray for Patrick, who must necessarily have been in far greater danger.

By the time the chariots reached the small slope of Slane, the evening looked as if it had been cut in two. Behind them to the west, Tara still stood clear and dark against the crystal sky, but beyond Slane, darkness had taken all the countryside. Thunder rolled and muttered like an angry beast that bellows for its freedom, and here and there the red fork of lightning split the black sky, lighting the darkness for one lurid second. At the foot of the Hill of Slane, Lucru seemed to make some effort to pull himself together. He stood up unsteadily in the swaying chariot and raised a hand.

"Stop here, oh King!" He looked upward at the hill that now loomed close, so close that they could no longer see the fire at the top, but only the glow that hung red and threatening above the dark masses of the trees. "Stop here, my King," Lucru cried, "and do not venture into the circle of his fire lest he should overcome you by the power of his magic!"

Leary was a realist and an intelligent man, as the Church of Rome had been at pains to find out, but he was not proof against the lifelong teachings of his Druids, and the religion he believed in. He, too, gazed uneasily up at the rosy glow above the hill, and bade his charioteer to halt. The following chariots swept up to form a circle around him, as if indeed it were to be a battle of swords and javelins.

"Go no nearer, oh King," Lucru cried again, and his voice was thin and hoarse. "Bid the man come down here and speak with you, and account for his actions."

In the strange, eerie light of the divided world, faces stood out pale and troubled from the growing darkness. They waited loyally on their King, but their superstitious minds were already trembling with the fear of the unknown; of the strange fire that lit the sky above their heads, and the unearthly darkness of the storm-split cloud behind the

hill. Leary stood up in all the colored splendor of his chariot, and looked around the ring of ashen faces for a mes-
senger.

"Who will go for me," he said to them, "and bring this
man?"

There was a long uneasy silence in which the thunder
rolled and threatened, and frightened eyes turned upon
each other, and no man offered. After a few moments,
Kiann leaped from the second chariot, and the storm light
was almost green on his pale hair. He looked all around in
contempt at the frightened faces of the men who would not
move, most of them warriors trained.

"I will go for you, my King," he cried. "Gladly I will go
for you. And the Roman will come with me, do not fear."
Several of them took courage then and shouted out that
they would go with him. He dismissed them with a gesture.
"I will go alone," he cried, and did not look back at them,
walking out through the chariot ring, and across the stretch
of grass to the gloom of the trees.

Leary watched him, and one red eyebrow lifted to his
hair, and he recalled with interest that he had sent this
young man once before to deal with Patrick, and he had
come back to say he found no reason for his death. He made
no remark on this, but watched Kiann vanish into the thick
darkness, and then waited in silence and patience for him
to come back, knowing without even turning his head of
the trembling and the shaken terror that ringed all around
him in the other chariots. By the Four Winds, he thought
with contempt, what do they think the Roman can do to
them, when he is not even a Druid. But he was honest
enough to acknowledge to himself that he had obeyed
Lucru at once when he told him not to go within the circle
of the fire.

The dense black cloud was now almost immediately
above Slane, blotting the light from the sky as if it were a

drawn curtain. Great drops of rain began to fall, blown in the rising wind, and now the lightning flared constantly over the ring of terrified faces. In the sharp flashes of sudden light, Lucru looked as if he had been resurrected from the dead, so sharp and pallid was his face, with the sweat standing in glistening beads on his waxy skin. In a moment of uncanny silence when the thunder ceased, they could hear the noise of Kiann and the Roman priest, thrusting their way downward in the pitch darkness that now wrapped the woods.

Almost before Leary knew of it, Patrick was before him, standing quietly outside the ring of shields and chariots so that the clear light which still hung to the west fell on his face, and blazed in the adze head of his Bishopric. Beside him stood a young boy, whose bright eyes roamed in curiosity over all the strange scene before him, and rested long on the bright figures of Leary and his Queen. Kiann did not return to his position in the chariot ring, but stayed outside it, standing with the Roman and the boy. To the already frightened eyes that watched them, they looked something more than mortal in the unearthly light of that strange evening, coming from the dark woods and standing there so still and silent; the bright-eyed boy, and the Bishop in his blaze of gold, and the tall young warrior with the green light tangled in his hair.

Lucru was the first to gather himself together, and it was easy for him to find his rage again, faced for the first time by the man who threatened all his inheritance of power.

"Who are you, Roman?" he screamed, and his hand flew up to clutch his chest as though his anger hurt him, and the lightning lit the sweat that was running down his face. "Who are you, that you dare to challenge the beliefs of Erin, and the orders and wisdom of its King?" The thunder dropped and they could hear the thin whistling of his breath. "Who are you, and who is your authority? Answer! Answer the High King!"

The last words died away on an anguished gasp, as if the Druid had no breath left to shout with. Patrick answered in the words he used to Dichu, and all eyes were on his face, ignoring Lucru, who clawed at his chest and struggled for his breath unnoticed.

"I challenge your beliefs," the priest said, and looked only at Leary. "I challenge your beliefs by the authority of my gracious God, whose ambassador I am in the land of Erin."

Lucru lifted his agonized face and summoned his whistling breath.

"A curse upon your god," he screamed. "A curse upon him and all—"

His words were lost and drowned in a massive roll of thunder and a blaze of purple lightning as the storm broke overhead. The last shred of light was extinguished by the black mass of storm cloud, with hail flailing down in white stinging torrents, rattling off the chariot sides and lashing the horses until they reared and pranced and tore at their harness, terrified by the thunder that crashed overhead with the noise of a thousand judgments. It was too much for the nerves of Leary's men, strained by the sacrilege of the distant fire, and terrified of this man who might command a magic stronger than their own. They did not stop to reason that such a storm had obviously been raging in the distance for many hours. One flaming fork of lightning split the thundering dark to show them Lucru, their magical defender with all the powers to keep them safe, himself collapsed into a heap of sodden robes in the center of their ring. Beyond it the Roman still stood unharmed and tranquil, with the rain streaming down his lifted face as he thanked his God for the storm which proved so good and opportune a weapon against magic and superstition.

The men in the chariots waited for no more when they had sighted the dead Lucru, stricken, they were certain, by the greater magic of the Roman. They forgot their King and they forgot their orders. They forgot that they were gathered in a circle, and drove forward without thought for anybody else, lashing their horses into a frenzy. The quick, brief storm was passing, and there was no longer even lightning to give them help. In the pitch darkness horse ran into horse and chariot poles splintered like dried reeds. Wheel wrenched off wheel, and side panels cracked away in rending wood and the screaming of curses, while the terrified horses neighed and scrambled and trampled on the poor wretches thrown from the chariots in the panic.

"The King and Queen!" cried Kiann at Patrick's side, and vanished down into the noise and confusion.

It was only a matter of minutes before the wild, freakish storm and darkness had come and gone. The space below the trees was strewn with bodies and the tumbled fragments of broken chariots heaped in the white glitter of the hailstones, while frenzied horses galloped away into the distance, their broken traces trailing behind them. To one side stood Leary with his Queen clinging to his arm. They were unharmed, having been in the center of the ring, so that the panic-driven chariots had collided with each other before they reached them. Water streamed from their hair and clothes and the Queen wept with fright. Even Leary looked pale, as though he held to his calm and dignity with an effort. Kiann held the horses of their chariot, talking to them and soothing them into quietness, and in among the tangled wreckage Lucran bent over the body of his fellow Druid.

In a moment he threaded his way over to the King, and he glanced at Patrick on the way with a mixture of terror and cold hate.

"He is dead, oh King!"

In silence, the eyes of the King and Queen turned on Patrick, and Benet looked from one to the other, a little dazed and not really quite sure himself whether his beloved Father had slain the Druid by magic or not. He was not concerned. In his own time, Patrick would explain it all, and he had no doubt it would be God's work. Leary dragged his fascinated eyes away from the priest and made an attempt to assert his position and be logical.

"What killed him?" he asked. "Was he struck by a chariot?"

"He is unmarked, my King, and he was there lying stricken before the chariots moved. I saw him." Leary was silent. He had seen him too. "Indeed," went on Lucran, "he was stricken at the very moment that he saw the fire of sacrilege on this hill. I saw this myself. It is magic, oh King, evil magic that could reach across the plain and strike your Druid with the touch of death! It is magic that will destroy your land. Kill, oh King! Your Avenger is beside you. Bid him draw his sword!"

Kiann turned his head sharply from the horses, but before he could speak, the Queen rushed forward from Leary's side, to throw herself down at Patrick's feet, indifferent to the cold of the long wet grass where the hailstones lay thick and white among the roots. Her nerves were not as strong as her husband's or her Druid's. She had seen all she wished to see of this man's magic and the things that it could do.

"Oh man," she begged and lifted her clasped hands in supplication. "Oh man, righteous and mighty, do not destroy the King, for the King will come, and kneel and worship thy Lord."

The priest had stood unmoving and in silence above the chaos. Now he looked down at the kneeling Queen and his face was gentle. True dusk was coming now, and there was no light in the golden disc as he bent to raise her up.

145

"You honor him," he said, "that you would so protect him. But make no rash promises on his behalf."

He looked into her agonized and fearful face as he helped her to her feet with her sodden hair plastered flat and dark around her cheeks and the water dripping from her cloak. He thanked his God that the first weapon offered to his hand had been sufficient to capture the Queen. This was a beginning. But when he looked at Leary over her bent head, he realized that the battle there was far from over, and that her promise of a subservient King was indeed a rash one. In the failing light it was to be seen that Leary had pulled himself together, and his proud eyes showed no sign of bowing down to worship anybody's Lord, but they did show a cautious and calm appraisal of the man who faced him in the falling darkness. Like Benet, he was not quite sure how they had been achieved, but the results of this man's work were plain here for everyone to see. He glanced once more at the carnage at the foot of the hill, and the sprawled body of his dead Druid.

"I care for no new gods," he said. "I am well pleased with the ones I have always known. But I bid you welcome to visit me in my Palace of Tara." By his side, Lucran swelled with fury and opened his mouth to shout his objections, but Leary spoke again before he had found words. "There," he said, "you can dispute this all more fully with my Druids."

The priest did not answer at once. His head bent as if grown suddenly weary under the weight of the golden disc.

"I will come tomorrow," he said then.

In his heart he groped humbly for adequate words with which to thank his unfailing God, who with one wild storm, and a sudden death, had gained him the entry into Tara.

On the Hill, Macha had slipped away from her mother in the crowds that roamed about and talked and speculated and watched and waited, staring over the plain to the Hill

146

of Slane, telling each other they could see this or that by straining their eyes into the evening shadows. The sudden, blinding storm dispersed them to shelter, and Macha with them, but over Tara it had lost its violence and was quickly past, so that she could creep out again from Micorta. She was there to listen on the fringes of the crowd when word passed from lip to lip of the frantic horses stampeding home, trailing their broken traces and the shattered fragments of their chariots; one even dragging the terrible remnants of a driver whose foot had tangled in the leathers. Desperately she stared in the growing darkness at the small steady light on the Hill of Slane, and desperately now she prayed to her new God. Even as she prayed, she could not find words to know if it were Kiann or the Roman that she prayed for.

Preparations were made at once to send out a party of warriors to search for Leary and his Queen, but it was full darkness when pin points of torchlight heading for Tara across the plain raised the excitement of the watchers once again. Macha turned and lifted up the skirts of her blue gown, running for Caher Crofin and slipping there into a place close in the shadow of the great gates. If it was the King, then he would come here, and also all those who were with him. She would be able to see them clearly in the torchlight about the gate, and close to, so that she could see if they were wounded—or anything; or if they had taken Patrick a prisoner.

In the blaze of light before the gates, she saw Kiann perfectly, riding in the King's chariot. There was only one other left of all the chariots that had gone out, and in this one rode the Queen. They were all sodden wet and much disheveled, and the Queen looked pale and shattered and as if she had been weeping, while the King stared straight in front of him but seemed to be seeing nothing. Beside him sat his Avenger, even dirtier and more tattered than when he had fought through the masses in Micorta. But under his wet, bedraggled hair his face looked calm and happy and a small smile touched his mouth.

Now Macha was ready to go home. Satisfied, she slipped away into the cold night, and after a while she began to skip, exactly as she had done on that first morning so long ago when Sescnen had told her she was to come home; small dancing steps that set the bright hair bobbing on her back and soon needed a happy humming to keep them properly in time. She did not remember at the moment that she was promised to the God of Patrick.

Chapter Fourteen

All through the night, the people of Tara did not go to sleep. They crowded around the hearth fires of their dwellings, marveling at the things which had happened that evening and endlessly discussing what they might mean; wondering and speculating about this strange Roman over on the Hill of Slane, who had made magic so strong that he had even contrived the death of a Druid, and brought darkness to the earth which had destroyed seven chariots and their occupants. As the hours of the early morning wore on, they heaped fresh turf on their fires and huddled even closer, feeling the ever-increasing cold of the night outside creeping even into their packed dwellings.

Over on the Hill of Slane, Patrick bade Manach work ceaselessly in his search for firewood. He lifted his head and seemed to sense the bitter air.

"It will be colder yet," he said, "before the dawn. There will be heavy frost now, and maybe for days to come."

"So late, my Father?" asked Coemen plaintively, rubbing his frozen hands. "So late? It is almost the month of May."

Patrick turned to him in the shifting firelight.

"Did we not have hail today? And bitter cold for many days? Do not complain, my brothers, for our bitter weather, like last night's storm, may prove to be the best of our friends."

Through the night Manach toiled to keep the fire high and blazing, to give them what warmth they could hope for in the icy wind on the open hillside, and cheerfully Benet helped him, coming and going quietly through the circle of sleepers with his thin arms full of brush. When at last there was wood well stacked to last the night beside the blazing fire, Manach did as Patrick had bidden all the others, and lay down huddled in his cloak as close as he could safely get to the heat of the flames.

Patrick alone sat apart and did not sleep, keeping his vigil for the great opportunity his God had offered him on the next day, and Benet came away from the others and took his place at Patrick's feet, knowing what he was about, and trying to keep awake for the night of vigil like his master. They were well beyond the warmth and shelter of the fire, so that when the scarlet morning crept across the sky with all the icy brilliance of deep winter, their clothes were white with frost, like all the tender grass and the small withered flowers and the young buds on the stricken trees, in this fantastic Spring.

They knelt for their Mass in the stiffened grass, and Coemen had to thaw the wine in front of the fire before it could be poured into the chalice held gingerly in Patrick's frozen fingers. He stood afterward warming himself, holding out his aching hands to the flames, with his eyes ever resting on the high bulk of Tara.

"Leary," he said thoughtfully to those around him, "is intelligent and reasonable." He chafed his fingers against the agony of returning life. "But he is also frightened, and fear casts out the best of good sense."

They looked at him, not understanding, simple men unable to follow his line of thought. Immediately he looked apologetic, as he so easily did.

"Forgive me my brothers. I speak my thoughts aloud and they are not clear to you as they are to me. What I mean is this. If the High King and I were to meet in quietness face to face, I do not doubt we would have much to say to each other, and could easily agree. But even Leary is slave for long years to his pagan priests, and last night he was truly frightened by the storm that our good and helpful God provided in our hour of need. Because he was frightened, his own good sense will have deserted him, and he will be as convinced as the Druids that I slew the other Druid and all those men with the strength of my magic powers." He looked around at them with his odd, deprecating smile. "I," he said apologetically, "who have no powers at all for anything, except those that God may place into my hands. But Leary does not know this, and in his fear I think he may try to dispose of me before I ever reach the walls of Tara." He turned to those who listened. "So I have formed a plan. Odran, you will take my chariot, and go slowly alone along the road to Tara. Wait for me below the walls, and do not fear for yourself. I am the only one they want. The remainder of us will go across the plain in secret, keeping to cover. Then, when we are met we will all go together into Tara, for I do not think that the King would try to kill me publicly, lest he brand himself afraid before his people."

Beside the dying fire they helped him into all the formal robes of his Bishopric, putting away the coarse woolen garments which he used for traveling. He fitted the band of the blazing adze around his forehead and took his crozier in his hand, and coming down through the dark woods he set out with his seven companions and the young Benet, across the frost white fields and the frozen streams, to face with the strength of God all the earthly might of the High King of Erin, and the magical powers of his Druids.

They proceeded slowly and carefully, keeping to the shelter of the woodland which partly covered the plain, and hearing the thunder and rattle of the chariot as it lumbered over the frozen ruts of the small road away to their left. Being small and quick, it was Benet's place to move on ahead, parting the bushes to watch for any sign of danger, while close behind him came Coemen, holding to the two great wolfhounds which Dichu had given to Patrick as the promised parting gift.

They were not very far on their journey when Patrick's caution was shown to be rewarded. Benet slipped suddenly back through the trees to the others, his fingers to his lips and gesturing away over toward the road. Silently, they all moved forward as he led, and saw in the middle of the bushes and thorn trees that fringed the edges of the road a warrior of the King's Household standing with his back to them, his yellow tunic brilliant in the dark bushes, and a primed bow held ready in his hand. Oblivious of the eyes that spied on him from behind, he obeyed his Captain's orders and kept a close and steady watch on the road, ready to let his arrow fly at the first sight of his victim; a little puzzled by the empty chariot with no one in it but the driver, which had already trundled slowly past him.

Patrick stared at him through the bushes, and wondered for a fleeting moment if the man who had ordered his death in this fashion was the fair young fellow who had tried it once before on the Hill of Dichu, who had come to him again last night with such courtesy and respect, to lead him to Leary at the bottom of the hill.

"There will be more of them," he said then. "They will be all along the road, lest the first should miss me. We must go in a little from the road, or they might hear us."

Cautiously, they moved as quietly as possible farther from the road and continued on their cold and difficult journey, and after a long weary time they came at last to the edges of the woodland, where only the frozen fields, spotted with a herd of restless deer, lay between them and the standing stones of Tara. They stopped at the edges of the trees and begged Patrick to go no farther, for there was no cover but the occasional bush or clump of thorn, and he could easily be seen if any of the watchers on the road should chance to turn; a comfortable bow shot and an easy target.

Patrick did not seem to be listening to their pleas. First he looked long and thoughtfully at the deer, and then he lifted his head and sniffed as though he was searching for the wind.

"We are down-wind from them," he said at last, and the others looked at him and did not understand. "That is why they have not scented us—and we have been very quiet. Three," he said then, "five, seven, eight, and a fawn. God is very good to us. With His mighty help and the good dogs of Dichu, the next weapon in the battle of magic is at hand."

They looked as if they thought the long cold night had frozen up his senses, or the long hand of Lucru had perhaps reached out from some world of the Druid spirit, to touch away his wits. But Patrick looked back at them with a grin of almost pure mischief on his face.

"My brothers," he said. "Those long days of my slavery tending sheep have not been wasted. Our good and generous Lord gives me now the things I learned there, to use against our enemy. Now look and listen carefully as I bid you."

They looked and listened, and gradually his own grin spread all across their faces, even to the dignified countenance of Coemen, who valued his position and did not think mirth became him. The young Benet clapped his hands across his mouth to suppress a yelp of delighted laughter.

"Do not hope too much," Patrick said warningly, looking at their amused faces. "They may well scatter. It will all depend on these fine creatures that I have here from Dichu."

The deer in the fields in front of them were much spread out, searching for something to eat in the cold, untempting grass. The main herd was scattered widely over to the right of where Patrick stood with his companions, but a small group, in their search for food, had drifted away to the left. The men counted them, exactly as Patrick had done. Eight deer—and one small fawn that stood shivering in the shadow of its mother.

"You see, my friends?" Patrick whispered and they nodded happily, Benet still spurting with silent laughter. The priest handed him his crozier and then turned and took the dogs from Coemen, unhitching their long leather leashes, but they did not move from his side, tribute to Dichu's training, tense and stiff from their pointing noses out to their feathered tails. Then Patrick dropped his hand, and they were off as his gesture had directed them, streaking like brown flashes down the gap between the two groups of deer. The small group was closer, and panic took them. A moment they stood, drawn together, their fear and indecision clear to the watching men, and Patrick's face was warmed by a small smile of pleasure in the excellence of his dogs. Then he whistled, a low thin whistle that would attract no one but the hounds, and instantly they turned to their left, stampeding the eight deer and the scrambling, galloping fawn out through the trees and bushes to the road. Before the dogs could follow he whistled them again, and they turned in their tracks and came streaking back to his hands, trembling in the pleasure of their obedience, waving their plumed tails at his praise and caresses. In silent pantomime the others laughed and clapped their hands and slapped each other on the back, and Patrick smiled with them, leashing his dogs, and thanking his God for all the skills he had learned in the long years on the northern hill.

"Hush," he said in a few moments and lifted a hand to still them. From the road came the undisciplined shouts of astonished warriors, not without a note of fear. They could hear them ploughing through the bushes on to the road, shouting at each other to ask if they had really seen what they thought. Patrick looked well satisfied.

"They will go back in haste now to Tara," he said, "and to those who sent them, and report that nothing passed along this road today other than eight deer and one fawn. They will say the Roman magician has a magic great enough to turn himself and his company into animals. Added to what happened last night, they will begin to think the Roman may have better magic than their Druids, and that will do well for a beginning. We can teach them later that the Roman has nothing at all except the generosity of his God. Now we will go quickly, my brothers, across this open field, while the warriors are occupied."

In a small thicket before the standing stones and the first walls, they waited awhile to allow time for the news to have got back and spread around the people of the Hill. When at last they emerged from the trees suddenly, at the foot of the small road, there were those who screamed and ran on sight of them, and all those who gathered in curiosity around the waiting chariot grew pale and ran away, to watch in safety from a greater distance.

But out of all his company, Odran the Charioteer was not satisfied. He listened with admiration to the story of how Patrick had brought them in safety thus far by a clever trick, but he did not share the smiles and pleasure of the rest of the company, and he made it clear that he did not think that their master was yet safely into Tara. He gazed with creased, unhappy face up the long road that climbed the flank of the Hill, fringed with the faces of the curious who had come to watch the Roman magician driving into the Palace of their King.

"There is a way to go yet, my Father," he said doubtfully, "and it is not trees now that line the road."

Patrick said what he had said at the beginning of the journey, looking also upward at the road lined with the watching crowd.

"Leary would not have me killed here in a place so public," he said. "It would confess his fear. That is why he would have slain me in secret on the road."

Odran was not convinced.

"I have listened to them talking here, my Father. It may be that the King's orders are one thing, but there are others here afraid beside the King. Any one of those could lift a spear and put an end to his own terror. Or there are those who would seek favor with the King by doing what he himself is unwilling to do."

"I will not allow myself to be afraid, my good Odran," Patrick answered him. "Calm your fears for me, for I have faith in God, whose work is not yet finished here in Erin. In truth, until this day, it was barely begun."

Odran could not argue with this. He was a young man, thin and muscular from the holding of mettlesome horses over rough roads and trackless ground; not one of the company which had come with Patrick, but another new Christian from the Kingdom of Ulidia. His hair was thick and black, curling down his forehead over gray, intelligent eyes that looked at his master now with a sad and steady knowledge.

"Then in the name of our God, do this for me, my Father," he said, and laid the leathers of the chariot into Patrick's hands. "Do this for me. Drive the chariot to the King's house, and I will take the seat of honor at your side. But before we start, I beg your blessing."

They stared at each other in a long silence of knowledge, as though they both knew that this was something that had to be, and neither could escape it. The Bishop of Rome could not come creeping to the King of Erin. He must come openly, standing in his chariot for all to see, and Odran was offering himself as a shield. He knelt down in the cold, rutted road, with his dark hair ruffled by the wind, and in the bitter silence Patrick blessed him, the chariot leathers still gathered with his crozier in the other hand, before the subdued and wondering crowd.

It was at the crest of the holy Hill, where the wide road turned in along the walls of Micorta toward Caher Crofin, that the thrown javelin took Odran in the back, and he died where he sat, in the seat of honor with Patrick's crozier in his hand. When they halted the horses before the King's dwelling, it was Patrick himself who withdrew the weapon, and closed the sightless eyes before they carried him away. With the help of his unfailing God, and the love of Odran, he had come safely into Tara.

Chapter Fifteen

Rather to Patrick's surprise, he was not conducted to an audience with the High King straight away. Not, when he and his companions were led with civility to a Guest House, was there any mention of a meeting.

"Rest yourself, Roman, and your companions, and warm yourselves after your cold journey. I will tell you of the High King's pleasure when he is ready to speak with you."

"And when will that be?" the priest asked, disconcerted

by his cool reception at the hands of the King, who had himself invited him here.

The Steward shrugged, and raised indifferent eyebrows.

"Who knows the mind of the High King until he himself is pleased to disclose it?"

With that, Patrick had to be content, and he comforted his offended companions by pointing out to them that far from planning hospitality for them, it had been Leary's intention that at this moment they should be grieving around his body somewhere on the road from Slane. It was a great victory that they were, instead of this, all inside the walls of Tara.

"It may be that shame strikes him now," he said, well aware of the importance of the laws of hospitality in Erin. He knew as well as they that to have planned the death of a bidden guest was the lowest treachery a man could stoop to, and beyond thought for a King. "It may be that he does not know how to face me."

The others nodded, but Patrick sensed their disappointment, and smiled round at them, the humblest and least troubled of them all. He lifted the gold band from his head, and rubbed a comforting finger around the red weal on his forehead.

"Come," he said. "We do the Lord's work, my friends, and we must do it at His pace, and not at our own. Let us make the best of all this comfort, while we may do nothing else. Indeed, my body begs for it."

He moved toward the cushioned benches around the fire, and beckoned the others to follow him, and the heat was grateful to their frozen hands and faces. Benet alone did not settle down with them, for he felt certain that Macha would come as soon as she was able, and he hung watchful around the entry to the Guest House, anxious to find out if his father might be on Tara for the Festival. There were a number of people gathered by the door in curiosity, waiting

for the Roman to reappear, and Benet moved among them
and listened to their talk. In a while, he went thoughtfully
back to his master beside the fire.

"My Father," he said. "Have you been bidden to the Feast
tonight? You are in Tara as an invited guest."

Patrick looked at him thoughtfully.

"The Feast?"

"There is the biggest Feast that Tara knows this evening,
after darkness falls, for the Festival of Spring. I have been
listening to those gathered round the door. If you are here
as the guest of the High King, why are you not bidden to
the Feast?"

The members of his Household began to exclaim again
indignantly among themselves, but Patrick did not seem to
take affront. His face was thoughful and somber.

"That is truth, my son," he said to Benet. "If I am here as
a bidden guest, why is there no chair for me at the King's
Feast? Could it be that they do not expect me to be able to
come?"

He would explain no more to their puzzled questions, re-
assuring Benet that there was still plenty of time for him to
be invited, and the boy wandered away again to the gates
to watch for Macha, brushing against a servant who came
in as he went out. The man carried a platter on which stood
one large crystal goblet of red wine. Ignoring all the others,
he demanded to be brought before Patrick, to whom he
held out the platter with respectful salutation.

"My master, Lucran the Druid of the High King, sends
his courteous greetings to the Roman, and offers a drink of
this, his finest wine."

Patrick still looked tired and cold, and the red band of
pressure from his golden disc was clear and painful-look-
ing around his weary forehead. He looked down at the cup
of wine and sighed deeply, as if it demanded of him some
effort he was disappointed to have to make.

"I thank your master, Lucran," he said carefully, "and bid you tell him that I will enjoy his gift when I am ready." He took the goblet, looking at it closely, and put it down on the table at his elbow.

The servant looked bothered, as though things were not going as they ought.

"My master," he said uneasily, "bade me watch you drink it."

"He did?" asked Patrick with interest. "Well, tell your master that I will drink it in my own moment and alone. You can go."

Still the man hesitated, looking from one to the other of them as if he did not know what to do.

"It is enough," Patrick said again, and Macc Cairthinn rose quietly from his seat and placed his mighty bulk close by the servant without word or threat. The man looked up at him just once, and then ducked his scared face and scuttled out of the room.

"He will have to tell his master," said Patrick with a small smile, "that the Roman was not thirsty." Carefully he picked up the goblet, and sniffed at it, and turned it in his hands in the light of the fire, and slowly shook his head. "It shows nothing," he said. "It shows nothing. Here Coeman," he said then. "Take it and place it outside the door. Carefully, and do not spill a drop. Place it on the ground outside the door, where it will get the full touch of the frost."

Coeman looked at him reproachfully.

"My Father," he said, "it would be better to drink it while it is still warm. You are chilled, and it would do you good."

"Yes, Coemen." Patrick smiled a little again. "But I fear it might not truly bring me much warmth. Now do as I bid you."

Still mystified, Coemen did as he was told. When he came back to the circle around the fire, Patrick said to them that he was going to sleep awhile, to pass the hours of waiting. "We had small sleep last night," he said, "and we need the clearest of brains for our encounter with the King."

"Where is the boy?" Patrick asked as he left the fire, unused to even one hour without Benet at his side. Manach the Firewood Man was able to answer.

"I saw him," he said. "I saw him, Father, when I sought the turf stack. He is at the gates of the dwelling, watching for his foster sister. Will I bring him to you?"

Patrick frowned a little and looked anxious, then he cleared his face deliberately.

"Leave him," he said. "Leave him. He may have his work to do here as well as I. He will come to no harm." He turned away into his bed space to sleep.

All over Tara the atmosphere was unsettled; unlike the usual gaiety of the Spring Festival when, with all the long rituals over, the people passed this last day in lighthearted sports, waiting for the mighty feast that would take place in the evening. In and around the Banquet Hall, Micorta, the preparations for this alone were going on as though nothing were afoot. Inside the huge room, the Stewards and the Footmen moved about their terrifying task of seating the thousand guests in order of their rank and precedence, a shield to mark each chair, knowing that one small mistake could mean an insult and a drawn sword, and blood on the King's hearth. The air was filled with the clamor of irritated arguments and risen voices, and of all the people in Tara, the rushing workers had too much to think of to give any heed to the stories of the Roman, or to fear them.

But out all over the Hill, the people gathered in whispering, frozen groups, too curious and anxious to go home to their dwellings and warm themselves at their fires; watching in wondering silence for signs of further magic. No one had seen the High King today, or any of his family, since they had come driving home, sodden, the previous evening. Yet it was whispered that Lucran this morning was in the highest spirits, despite the magical death of Lucru, assuring those about him that there was no further need to fear the Roman priest. They asked him if the Roman would be at the Feast that evening, and Lucran laughed so that his fleshy jowls trembled above his chin, and a deep congested flush covered his shaven head.

It was a couple of hours before Macha at last managed to come to Benet, who moved watchfully through the crowd outside the Guest House, disarming them with his open and unhesitating smile, and parrying gently and pleasantly all the questions that he could not answer.

"Macha!" He ran to her at once when he saw her, oblivious of all the eyes that turned to watch. "Macha! How happy a day! We are both together here in Tara, and our Father with us. Do you know if my own father is here?"

Macha was breathless, unable for a few moments to speak, holding to his hands with her eyes flying in pleasure all over his face.

"I have had to run away, Benet," she managed to say at last, "when my mother was busy. I always seem to have to do wrong for our Father! But I had to see you." She beamed with affection, gripping to his hands. "My father bade me stay at home and keep out of the crowds and leave the Roman to the King. He is furious that he has contrived to reach Tara, and he seems to think that he is beginning to influence Kia—other people besides me," she finished lamely.

"He is right, is he not?" Benet asked her. "Look about you!"

She answered his first question before she looked, her words tumbling out in her excitement and pleasure.

"Your father is not here, Benet. My father advised him to stay away from Tara for a while, even though the whole affair of my running away proved so easily settled."

Benet's face shadowed, but he shrugged philosophically.

"I thought he and my mother might have visited you for the Festival. Look at those people," he said again, as though willing himself not to think of his family.

Macha looked then at the silent, freezing crowd who stood in the bitter wind, troubled and uncertain and afraid to go to their homes. Many of their eyes were fixed fearfully on the boy and girl, as if they expected them at any moment to turn into ravens or other birds of terrifying ill omen.

"I did not mean that he was influencing them," she said, "but someone else. But he will gain all of them, too, in his own time. But Benet—" She drew him to one side in the shadows of the Guest-House door. "Benet, there are strange tales abroad today." She looked him up and down much as the crowd looked at both of them. "They say that you came from Slane in the shape of a fawn and all the men as deer. They say that it was magic. Patrick and his Church do not believe in magic. You know that."

Benet broke into his wide, infectious smile and then a burst of helpless laughter. He looked around at the staring people and his face sobered. "Listen," he said, and he told her then all that Patrick had told him and the others about fighting these people first with what seemed to be their own weapons, and then leading them to God when he had gained their attention and respect. Grinning again, he told her of the God-given gift of the group of eight deer and a fawn, which Patrick had used with his own experience as a shepherd. Macha smiled inside her hood.

"I wish that I could see him again," she said wistfully. "To speak with, and hear his voice."

"There is no reason not," said Benet. "He is no distant lord. But I think that he is sleeping now. Come, and we'll find out."

He left her at the Guest-House door while he went in to see if the priest could speak with her, and as she waited, her eyes caught sight of something on the ground outside the door, and puzzled, she bent to pick it up and was turning it in her hands when Benet came out to her again.

"They are all asleep," he said, "save Macc Cairthinn, who watches over them, and Manach, who watches over the fire. We will wait awhile. What is that you have there?"

"I don't know," Macha answered. "It is a strange place to leave a cup of wine, on the ground outside the door. Look, it has frozen solid!"

"Truly," said Benet, amazed, and took it from her, holding it upside down. "Someone must like their wine well chilled! Look, Macha, there is just one clear drop unfrozen at the bottom. How strange!"

All the great questions of Magic and the Roman Church and the powers of Patrick were forgotten, and the growing saintliness of Benignus. Their breaths rising as one vapor in the frosty air, and the red head pressed against the brown one, they bent, two fascinated children, over the upended wine cup outside the Guest-House door.

"Put it back, Benet," Macha urged then, "and let's see if it freezes the whole way down."

Carefully he replaced it where she had found it, and they smiled at each other in conspiracy.

"I am going back home now," Macha said. "Yes, Benet, it is better," she added to his gesture of protest. "I do not want to anger my father too much. I will try and come again when the Father is awake."

She was bitterly disappointed not to have seen him, longing as she had done through all the tedious year to be able to see him again and speak with him of the things that troubled her and of the decision she was being asked to make. But in that lonely year she had grown older. She was no more the thoughtless child who had danced in the waves below the dun of Sescnen. The long year in her father's house had taught her patience, and that there are some things that are best gained slowly.

"There will be a better moment," she said, "and I can come back. And who knows, but tonight at the Feast, he may gain the pleasure of the High King, and then we can all listen to him in peace."

Benet looked at her.

"He is not bidden to the Feast."

"Not bidden to the Feast? But he is an invited guest on Tara! The King invited him. Kia—a friend of my father's was there and heard him, in all the terror below the Hill of Slane."

"You have heard about all that?" For a moment he was distracted.

"I heard it all. I was in the Hall and listened while this friend told my father. My father is angry that Patrick has reached Tara, but I know that he is thoughtful, too, now, because he is a brehon and a just man, and always sees all sides." She came back to her first problem. "But why is Patrick not invited to the Feast?"

Benet shook his head, quite without understanding, and Macha slowly drew her blue hood close around her face. They stood in puzzled silence, baffled by something beyond them which they instinctively feared for their master, and then Macha touched Benet's hand helplessly in farewell and smiled at him, turning to run away along the ridge of the Hill. Benet went slowly back into the Guest House, to join Macc Cairthinn beside the fire.

It was well past noon when Patrick woke, and the brilliant day clouded over with a gray cold that blanched the faces of the watching people and ate through their warm cloaks and their woolen tunics and into the very marrow of their bones. The Plain of Meath lay stark and barren as in the very depth of winter, while up on the sacred Hill preparations were almost complete for the great Feast of Spring.

"Now," said Patrick when Macc Cairthinn had wakened all the others. "Now, Coemen, you will bring me back the goblet of wine. With great care, I beg you, Coemen."

Coemen was surprised. He had forgotten the wine, and could not see that it would be worth drinking now. However he went obediently to where he had set it down outside the door. As he came back to the fire, his face had almost the same childlike pleasure as had lit Benet's and Macha's. Like them, he held the goblet upside down.

"It is of little use, my Father," he said, giving it a shake. "See, it is frozen."

Patrick passed a hand across his face as if he could not bear the sight.

"Coemen, my brother, I said carefully," he remonstrated, and took it tenderly into his own hands. The frost was white and delicate on the crystal cup, and the wine inside it a faint, solid pink. Carefully and gently, Patrick turned it round and round a moment before the fire.

"Give me another goblet, Coemen," he said then, with his eyes on the one in his hands. The eyes of all the other men were on him in silence, puzzled, and not understanding what he did.

With the utmost care, he upended the slightly thawed goblet above the empty one which Coemen had put into his hand, and allowed the lump of pink, frozen wine to slide gently from one into the other. Quickly then he righted the first one, and in the red light of the fire, bent to stare into the bottom of it.

"Ah," he said, with satisfaction tinged with sadness. "Look, my brothers."

From hand to hand they passed the goblet, peering in without any further enlightenment at the drop of clear liquid which still lay unfrozen at the bottom of the vessel. Dumbly they gave it back to him and waited for him to explain. A moment he sniffed at it, wrinkling his nose in distaste, and then smiled all around at them.

"It is something more," he said, "that my generous God taught me in the days of my slavery. All my days have been in preparation for this one in His eternal mind. I observed many times when I was out with my sheep in weather such as this, that if I had with me water and milk in two vessels, they did not freeze at the same moment. A greater cold was needed to make solid of the milk. So I felt that if poison lay at the bottom of this cup, God might grant it to me that it would freeze more slowly than the wine, and so reveal itself, thus showing me the mind of Lucran and the King."

He looked around their appalled and outraged faces, and now his own was serenely cheerful.

"No wonder," he said, "that there is no place laid for me at the Feast tonight. I am not expected to be present."

He stood up, his eyes alight, and his whole being alert to the challenge.

"Go now, Coemen, and bar the door," he said. "Refuse all comers, and offer any who may see you a face of grief. Tell no falsehoods, but let the thought reach Lucran that he has been successful. Let the word creep all over Tara that the Roman is dead."

Chapter Sixteen

Coemen did his work well, presenting a face of grief-stricken silence to any who appeared before the wicket of the Guest House, refusing to open the door and saying sadly that his master was unable to receive any visitors.

News flew so rapidly that, by the time evening came, the whole sacred Hill was ready to regard the coming Feast as a celebration of the High King's victory over the Roman, who was not it seemed, for all his magic, powerful enough to resist Leary and his clever Druids. Lucran's face was broad with satisfaction, feeling certain that he had driven Rome for all time out of the land of Erin. In Caher Crofin, Leary stretched his long legs out in front of him and sighed, and shouted for Fergus to bring his board. He was more far-seeing than Lucran, and knew that Rome would not be defeated by the killing of one man. He sighed again, but this time a little regretfully. If he had to make peace with Rome, and in the end he thought he had to, and let her bring her faith to Erin, he would as soon have treated with this man as any other. He responded to his quiet and steadfast air, and found him worthy of respect. Well, it was done now. He turned his attention to the men being set along the board by the quivering fingers of Fergus.

When Labran brought the news home in the early evening, Macha rushed at him and clung to his sleeve.

"Oh no, my father! Oh no, it is not true! Surely it is not true! How did he die?"

Labran looked faintly puzzled.

"No one seems to know exactly that, my daughter, but the word has gone round, and any who have tried to visit with him this late day have found the doors barred, and the man who opens the wicket stricken with grief."

He turned and rubbed his hands cheerfully before the blazing fire.

"Ah," he said, "how welcome! What weather for a Festival of Spring. Well, Bres, my wife, it will be a great banquet of celebration tonight. The man from the sea is dealt with, and we can all be easy. I tell you, there were many beginning to listen to him after last night."

Carefully, he did not look at Macha, determined not to recognize that Patrick's death should be any particular grief to her. Only Bres looked at her, and felt her heart wrench with pity as she caught for one moment the despairing and horror-stricken gaze of the tawny eyes, before the girl turned and ran, blindly and without a word, seeking the privacy and silence behind her bed curtains in the grianin. She did not weep, dumb and shattered in her grief for Patrick himself, done to death by these capering Druids, for she was quite certain that Lucran was in some way responsible. Overlaying her grief was the panic knowledge that now there would be no one to advise her. With every time that she set eyes on Kiann, his fair head rising above those all around him, it grew more difficult to remember that she had promised to give her life to the God of Patrick. She knew now in her heart that no matter what her parents wished, she herself desired this marriage more than anything else on earth. But she could not escape the feeling that it was weakness to turn her back on her first vow, betraying surely the God she had promised herself to? It was not even as if Kiann was a Christian, or could ever be one, now that Patrick was dead, for God would die now as Patrick had done on the Hill of Tara, and in all Erin, and there would be no more Christians.

She looked at her marriage in despair. It could have been so splendid, but now she felt it would be clouded forever by her broken promise. She was still sitting there when Bres came to her, dressed splendidly for the Feast, gleaming with silk and gold.

"Ah, my Macha, do not sit there fretting your heart away. There is so much to see tonight. Let me send one of the bondmen to take you up to watch the guests enter Micorta for the Feast. You would like that?"

She shook her head to all her mother's coaxing, and pressed back into the shadows of her bed, and her mother gazed at her despairingly. Alive or dead, this priest of Rome gave them no peace in their house. She had to turn away. There was no time to argue with the girl, or she might delay Labran at the Feast, and woe betide any guest who was not in his or her place to rise in homage as the High King entered.

Macha watched her mother go out, and past her through the opening door she could see the night sky scarlet against the bitter stars, blazing with the firelight and candlelight of the feasting King.

The long frenzied hours of preparation were over, and Micorta lay ready for the Feast. The guests gathered in ranks outside the fourteen open doors, sealed only with a cord of scarlet silk and the tasseled spears of tall warriors, waiting for the blast of trumpets that would sear the night to proclaim the Feast begun. They waited there to take their places up to the number of ten hundred, shivering in their gorgeous clothes in the wind that tore across the Hill; Kings and Lesser Kings and Chieftains, and Nobles from the First down to the Fifth Grade; Judges and Soothsayers and Shipwrights and Poets from the First Grade down to the Grade of Six; Deerstalkers and Fort builders, Charioteers and Champions, Druids and Drummers, and Engravers and Flute Players; Builders and Physicians and Chess Players, with the brooding face of Fergus at the head of these, shuffling in to crouch abstracted above his platter.

When at last they were all seated in their appointed seats and the trumpets died on the wind, Leary came with a fresh fanfare to take his place, brilliant with all the splendor of his Kingship, the sheen of gold about his neck and wrists and banded in the dark thickness of his long red hair. His Queen beside him looked pale and troubled, as if she had not slept, and felt burdened by the weight of her flowing gown and the heavy gold fillet around her brow. Leary did not seem to share her anxieties. He looked forward with great content to this Feast that was properly for the Festival of Spring, but would be tonight for him, and all Tara, the celebration of the defeat of the Church of Rome.

The whole gay company was lighthearted with the release from fear which they did not even understand, and talk rose like last night's thunder when the King was seated, battering back and forth across the laden tables as the servants scuttled from the kitchens with great steaming platters, and the red wine and golden mead flowed into goblets that were emptied almost in the moment they were filled. The roar of conversation and the plangent music of the harps and flutes poured out with the light into the dark night outside, drowning all sound of anyone who might be approaching along the Hill.

So it was that at the height of the Feast, Patrick came unnoticed and stood beside the Keeper of the Door. When he turned and saw the dead Roman standing in silence in the candle glow, with the light on the pale silks of his cope and shining from his forehead, he could do no more than open and close his terrified mouth and cling to the door pillars for support for his stricken knees; at his side the guardian warriors leaned petrified on their spears, and forgot to bar the way.

He was in the middle of the Common Hall before he was noticed, and then conversation died on gasps of terror, until all down the seven hundred feet of Micorta there was no sound save the whisper of startled feet in the rushes and the small clatter of a spilt goblet or a dropped platter. Lucran, now Chief among the Druids, rose halfway to his feet as if he had the strength to rise no further, and his face was as pale and waxen as that of Lucru in the moment of his death, but from out of all the thousand guests, only one man stood up to do him honor. From the same exalted table as Lucran, the Chief Poet of Erin alone came to his feet, and looked in silence at Patrick across the dumfounded heads with his hands crossed in submission and respect. Patrick looked back at him and blessed him, and silently thanked his God for his first convert on the Hill of Tara. Then he turned toward the King.

Leary recovered himself more quickly than either his Druids or his guests.

"We did not expect you, oh Roman," he cried across the silent hall, and Patrick's eyes gleamed a moment, knowing why. "But now you are come," went on Leary, "sit with us and share our Feast, you and your companions. Stewards, seat our guests!"

The Stewards ran here and there and fussed through the hall, until all were seated according to their dignity and rank. Patrick came serenely and took his place close beside the King, and while the remainder of the long meal lasted they spoke nothing to each other except formal words of empty courtesy, watched by a restless and anxious Lucran from across the room. But on the cleared tables, when the food was swept away, Leary banged his fist against the noise of the harps and flutes and the squeals of the tumbling clowns and shouted for Lucran.

"Come, Druid," he said, "and sit close beside me here with this Roman, and let me hear your dispute. Set yourselves here one against the other, and argue out your gods! Let me listen!"

Through the long hours of the hot, noisy night they disputed before Leary against the background uproar of the Feast, Lucran in ferocity and anger and more than a little of the fury of fear; Patrick serene and determined, stating quietly the incontestable truths of his faith. It was the cold, dark hour that waits on the dawn when Leary at last yawned hugely and stood up, giving the signal that the Feast was at an end.

"Words, words, words," he said to the two before him. "Let me see more than words. Let me see which is stronger by signs and happenings—the magic of the Druid, or the faith of the Christian, for you tell us Roman, that nothing that you do is done by magic."

Patrick begged his God to help him to see whatever weapons He might lay ready to his hand.

Outside Micorta the air was bitter still, but softened with a new dampness, and the first few flakes of snow feathered the black sky, drifting through the blaze of light beyond the doors. Immediately Lucran threw up his arms and raised his crested head to the sky.

"This is our god," he cried. "This is the power of the Elements, that brings for us the Black Wind from the north, laden with snow in the days of the Spring. The Winds are our servants, oh Roman, and will do as we bid them." With wide-flung arms he howled his incantations into the darkness to the North Wind, and the Lesser Druids gathered around and joined him, with the lights of Micorta behind them and the people pouring out in order, as they had gone in, from the fourteen open doors. The priest and his companions waited quietly and patiently until at last he stopped.

"Now," Lucran said, dropping his arms and turning to Patrick, and the light from the Hall shone in the heavy sweat on his face, so fierce had been his pleadings with the spirit of the weather. "Now, in this season of Spring, I have bidden the Black Wind of the North to cover all that plain with snow up to the depth of a man's boot!"

Patrick looked unimpressed. With one sniff at the wind, and a glance at the low-hung weight of the dark sky, he could have promised such a thing himself and thought it reasonable. But the massed watching people moved and muttered in awe and admiration, whispering together that it would take the Roman a great deal to better this. All the Roman did, however, was to express his unbounded admiration for the powers of Lucran, and then he turned away to his Guest House, saying that he would sleep now and see the snow for himself when it was light.

When he came back, it was late morning and the snow was as high as a man's boot and no longer falling. He and his Household had to gather up the hems of their robes to plough through it up to the crest of the Hill, where the triumphant Lucran waited for him, and with him a watchful Leary and his Queen.

"See for yourself then, Roman." The Druid almost spat at him. "See for yourself my power over the Elements. Why should we consider this timorous god of yours when the world itself is ours! Alone I have done this, in the season foreign to snow. Could you do it, oh Roman?"

Patrick looked at him pleasantly.

"Alone I could not do it. Without the help of my loving God, I can do nothing. Now, friend Lucran, prove your power to me a little more. You have brought the snow, you say, alone and by your own powers. Now with these same powers, let me see you make it go away."

There was a furious, astounded silence, and they glared at him and glared at each other, and looked to Lucran for a lead and he could not give it. In the group of Nobles behind the King, Labran gave a sudden gulp of laughter, then clapped his hands to his mouth and pretended a fit of coughing, and Kiann turned and looked at him in sharp surprise and not a little pleasure.

By evening the snow was there still, lying white and unmelting all across the plain, strange and improbable under the young leaves and the greening hedges. After many hours, the Druids had retired, surly and defeated, into their own rath, having failed to move the snow by any rite or ceremony or incantation which they could devise.

"And can *you* do it?" Lucran had yelled at Patrick in the end, almost dancing in front of him, his round, fleshy face alive with hate and malice. "Can you do it, priest of Rome?"

Patrick's pleasantness was unfailing.

"When my God wills," he said amiably, and retired once more behind his own walls.

Labran was still laughing to himself when he reached his own homestead in the evening.

"I cannot but have respect for this Roman," he said. "He is clever and intelligent, and keeps his temper, using his brains against the power-mad Lucran. He may well defeat · him yet."

Macha listened to him and her heart lifted to hear him speak so of Patrick, but she was careful now, lest she antagonize him again.

"My father," she asked gently, "why did you tell me he was dead?"

"Because I thought he was, daughter, and so did Lucran and indeed all Tara, until he appeared like a spirit in the middle of Micorta, with none seeing him come. Lucran in a moment of anger let slip that he had sent him a cup of poisoned wine."

"Oh!" cried Macha, and clapped her fingers to her mouth.

"What is it, daughter?"

She told them how she and Benet had found the frozen wine, and they were so interested in what she said that they failed to notice that she had gone to the Guest House against their wishes.

"So," cried her father, "the wine froze and the drop of poison did not, and he could separate the two. I admire him! He thinks, this Roman, and for this I admire him!"

Macha seized on what she thought to be a good moment.

"Well, my father, if he is not such an evil man, can I not go and see him? And listen to him speak? Must I stay shut within the rath all the days he is here? Please, my father, please!"

Labran looked down at the pale, unhappy face and found it difficult to forbid her anything. But in spite of his growing approval of the Roman, who had struck a chord of intellect in him, his daughter was to marry Kiann. He could not take the chance, until this was safely done, of

177

allowing her to come again within the influence of this clever and endearing priest, to whom he admitted even himself increasingly drawn.

"No my daughter," he said firmly. "No. It will be as I have ordered. You will not leave the rath while the Roman is on Tara, no matter what I have come to think of him."

Hopelessly she turned away and left them. If she could not see him, she did not wish to hear about him, thickening her loneliness and indecision. All she could tell herself now was that she could not help it, and if she had forsaken God, it was not of her own doing.

Up on the snow-covered Hill, darkness was falling, but Patrick still sat on a stool in the bitter cold outside the door of the Guest House, nor would he move inside for a moment, even to eat. Coemen came again to plead with him as it grew dark.

"My Father, come to the fire. You will take a fever in this bitter cold."

Patrick looked at him and laughed. "I took no fevers, Coemen, on the hill of Slemish, and many a night I spent there with my sheep in the winters, far more cold than this. No, my friend, I thank you for your care, but I must stay here and watch the night. It is magic at the moment that is needed to win them, and I must provide it. This is another weapon in the battle for their souls, and I cannot allow it to escape me. But take the boy."

He laid a hand on Benet, who shivered beside him in the bitter wind, and reluctantly the boy left him, and went inside with Coemen.

It was in the first gray light of morning, with the sky still hanging dark above the white expanse of the plain, that he stood up suddenly and called his company.

"Go, Coemen," said Patrick, and his voice was taut with urgency. "Go and bid Lucran and his Druids join me on the crest of the Hill. The King also if he will come, and all the people you can rouse. Go quickly."

He himself walked the trodden snow up to the crest, filling the silent dawn with the hollow booming of his bell, and by the time Lucran and his followers had arrived, and then Leary and his Court, a large crowd had gathered in the gray light, uncombed and sleepy, gathering their cloaks around them against the bitter cold. Patrick looked over them all. Can they not smell it themselves, he thought amazed; especially the Druids, who set so much store upon their knowledge of the weather; the change of wind, creeping steadily around in this last hour, so that at any moment there would be the first gust of warm, wet wind from the South West, probably bringing the sun, but at least, at this time of year, bringing a quick and certain thaw. Can they not feel it themselves, he thought again, and thanked God for their simplicity, through which they could be led to Him.

He stood above them, and in their listening silence, cried aloud to them all. "In the name of my God," he cried, "I will clear the snow, which your Druids have failed to do." Even as he spoke, he could feel the warm Spring wind freshening on his cheek, and he lifted his hand and blessed the plain, for was it not about to do God's work for him? Then he turned again to the gaping crowd.

"I will go now, and pray to my God," he said, "and in awhile I will come back to you, and we will see if I have succeeded where the Druids have failed."

He passed several hours in prayer and quietness, begging the help of his unfailing and generous God, and by the time he came back and stood once more before the people on the crest of the Hill, the soft, moist wind was blustering fiercely over the land, clearing the sky to a serene and tender blue, and patching the white fields already with melted stretches of young green grass. Almost every person on the Hill stood staring at the sky and the clearing plain, and the thatched roofs steaming in the sun, and muttering together in awe and consternation.

When Patrick appeared, they fell silent, their eyes resting on him with fear and wonder on all their faces. Into this silence came Leary, followed by his train of angry and defeated Druids, and like his people, he stood and looked long at clear blue sky and the snow vanishing from the plain. Then he turned and faced the priest, and his narrow, intelligent eyes were crinkled with amusement tempered with respect. Patrick met his gaze straight and steadfast, and did not waver. He knew in that instant that the High King understood well what he was doing, and regarded the contest with the Druids as one of brains and not of magic. Beside him, Labran's face echoed the same expression, his eyes warm and amused, but respectful, on the Roman. At last Leary spoke, looking from Patrick's imperturbable face to the sullen, heavy scowl of Lucran.

He waved a ringed hand at the fast-vanishing snow on the plain.

"I am moved to think," he said, and his voice was tart and dry, "that all this could have occurred with little help from either of you. I seem to remember that I have seen snow before, and seen it vanish also, in the sudden sun of Spring. I am not as simple as my poor people."

Labran's face split into a smile, as though against his will, and he watched Patrick with deep interest for his answer, as did the High King. But it was Lucran who answered, pointing his wand at Patrick with a hand that shook with anger and menace.

"True, true, oh King, as far as the Roman is concerned! I brought the snow, oh Leary, but he could not clear it until it went of its own accord. But I, Lucran, with the strength and wonder of my magic, brought it on the plain

180

in all the warmth of Spring. It is I who have proved the Roman false. Tell the people, oh King!"

Leary did not move to do so. With his eyes still on Patrick, he asked that they would show him some sign which would be a definite answer.

"I will do anything you wish, oh King," said Patrick, and begged for his God to help him to give some sign that this clever and clear-sighted King might be willing to accept. He felt that Leary had respect for him, and wavered to his side, but that he needed one more definite sign to confirm his mind.

Leary himself had an idea.

"Go down," he said, "to the Well of the Calf, and cast in both your Holy Books. See which of them will come out undamaged, protected by your faith."

"No," cried Lucran, before Patrick had time even to consider it.

"And why not?" Leary's eyes were fierce on the Druid.

"Because water is one of this man's gods. I have heard tell that when people are moved to his faith, he takes them to a well and pours water on their heads. He has control of the spirit of water, and could do as he wished with my Holy Book."

Patrick's company looked at each other and smiled at this Druid tale of baptism, and beside the priest Benet broke out into his clear, easy laugh. Lucran glared at him.

"I would engage you, Roman," he said to Patrick, "in a trial of fire. Let us cast our Books into the flames, and we will see which one will be preserved."

While he stood there, so easy and tranquil, leaning on his crook and listening to all that passed, Patrick had been thinking fiercely, and every thought tied with a prayer for help. This moment was his last chance. He must win Leary now, or never. He must gain his support and the freedom of his land, or he might as well walk off Tara now, and out of the land of Erin and leave it to its mouthing Druids. Nothing was too great to stake on this. He turned his face, and stood a long moment considering the strength and steadiness of the Spring wind on his face, and then he turned back at last to Lucran.

"I accept your challenge, Druid," he said calmly, "but I challenge you with more than a Holy Book at stake in the flames."

"What then?" asked Lucran suspiciously.

Patrick took a deep breath and trusted himself and all he was about to do to God's hands.

"We will build a small house," he said, and lifted his clear, commanding voice so that it encompassed all the people on the hill. "Half of it shall be built of green branches still wet from the days of snow, and the other half shall be built of dry timber from the timber store." He paused, and there was no sound over the curious crowd but the rush and tinkle of the melting snow, and the wild delirious singing of the birds who had been given back their Spring. "In the dry half," he continued, "I will go myself, and I will wear the cloak of a Druid. In the wet half, you will go yourself, wearing the cloak of my Bishopric, that we may be well confused. Let us then have the hut fired at the center, and see whose gods will give them protection."

Lucran glared at him a long time and did not speak.

"I do not trust you," he said then. "If it is you, you will take some advantage. Let it be someone else." He glared around, seeking whom Patrick might value most, and his eye fell on Benet.

"Put in the child," he cried triumphantly. "Put in the child, and I accept your challenge."

Patrick bent his head. "It is as you say," he said.

Lucran laughed as if he thought him touched, and even Labran and the King looked doubtful, glancing at the boy beside the priest.

"I will sit there," shouted Lucran, "and listen to the boy screaming as he roasts!"

For one moment, Benet looked up at Patrick anxiously, and the priest, without looking down at him, laid a hand on his shoulder. It was enough for Benet, telling him not to fear, and his handsome face resumed its normal tranquility.

"Let us build, let us build," cried Lucran, who could not get quickly enough to the business of the final defeat of this upstart Roman. "You may tell them how to build it." He laughed a high, excited laugh. "It will be the last thing you will do on Tara!"

The crowd was gathering closer and closer, and no one moved to hold them back, all eyes on the small structure that was being rushed up in the open space before the King. Labran looked troubled, and the face of the King was creased with doubt.

Patrick bade the men build the hut with its dry end facing to the wind, and all the time he was alert to every change in the air that blew now strong and fierce over the top of the Hill. Winds at this time of year could be changeable and gusty, and one swift veering at the wrong moment could bring him disaster. Silently, as he watched and ordered and directed, he begged help from the only One who could bring it to him here.

In a little while, the hut was ready, and Lucran was almost capering with pleasure and anticipation. He pulled off his striped cloak and draped it around Benet's shoulders, cackling with amusement at the small figure dwarfed and weighed down by the heavy, trailing garment.

"Good grave clothes for you, boy," he said. "Good grave clothes."

Benet only smiled and kept his eyes on Patrick, while Coemen came and lifted off the pale, heavy silken cope, and with a look of fine distaste, laid it at arm's length on the Druid's back.

"Benet, my son," said Patrick then, quietly. "You will do this for me?"

"For you, my Father, and for God."

"That is good. Put your faith in Him, and we have not any reason, either of us, to be afraid. If there is any danger to you, I will get you out, but I have faith in my helpful God, who will not leave us in this moment. When first the hut is kindled, it may be that burning fragments will fall on you from the roof. Beat them out at once and do not fear—that is all that should happen."

Lucran could not wait. He saw the overthrow of this presumptuous Roman immediate to his hands.

"Come boy, why do we delay? Are you afraid?"

Benet only smiled again, and Patrick blessed him. As he turned to go into the hut, his eye was caught by a sudden commotion in the edges of the crowd. Down in the rath of Labran, word had crept about that there were strange acts of mystery and magic going on up on the Hill between the Roman and the Druids. Macha watched the bondmaid who sat with her listening with widening eyes and open mouth to the whispered tale of another who had rushed in off the Hill. Guiltily the girl looked at Macha, and then made some excuse, and Macha leaped to watch them from the high windows of her grianin, pelting off along the paths of the rath as fast as they could run. There was not another soul in sight, as if suddenly the whole busy rath were peopled by the dead. Quickly she seized her cloak and made off after the two girls, expecting at every moment to be stopped, because her father had made his orders clear to all the Household. But the Household had fled like everybody else, to the high crest of the Hill of Tara, and the duel between the Roman and the Druids. The small wicket in the big gates stood open, and there was no one there to guard it.

Macha picked up her blue skirts and ran full pelt like everybody else toward the top of the Hill, no longer concerned about disobeying her father. With the Gate Keeper gone, she was the very least of it.

On all sides of her, people were running too. Those too busy or too indifferent to have gone before were hurrying now, on the rumor that had crept down to them from the Hill above. The Roman was about to burn the young boy who was one of his followers. At the crest of the Hill the crowd was solid. Blindly, she fought her way through the crowd, pinching, biting, pushing, and using every pressure she could think of to part the dense thickness of people and let her to the front.

But when she burst out at last, at the front edge of the circle, she had no breath to speak. All the bitter battle of the way up, she had been terrified for Benet, puzzling in blind misery as she fought her way along, as to why the gentle Patrick, who so loved the boy, should do this thing. Even as her disheveled head thrust itself through the last pair of elbows, she saw her fears needless, and knew that she could save what little breath she had. Benet was in no danger.

Whatever Patrick was doing with him, she knew at once that it was nothing harmful. They moved side by side toward a small, strange hut, made half of fresh green branches, and half of dry wood, like any other house. On her beloved Benet's face there was the customary smile of sweet confidence with which he approached all the concerns of his Father in God. Her noisy arrival at the crowd's edge attracted his attention just as he was about to step into the hut, and he turned and saw her; then in that last moment, his smile was for her alone. Peace took her, and in the wondering, fearful crowd, she stood as quiet and tranquil as Benet himself, waiting for what might come.

Lucran was first into the hut, twitching at Patrick's cope

of creamy silk, his heavy face self-satisfied and certain of his victory. Behind Benet on the dry end, Patrick closed the door, and immediately the boy began to sing; all the hymns and psalms he knew, to praise his Lord who would protect him through this ordeal. Sweet and true and peaceful, like the blackbirds in the budding trees, the boy's voice floated out over the crowd, and with one last considering cheek turned toward the wind, Patrick reached out and took a blazing torch from the hands of Coemen.

"Is there a just man here," he cried, "who will light this fairly in the middle, and take no side."

The vast crowd was frozen as if death had taken them where they stood, eyes rooted on the torch in the priest's hand, and there was no sound but Benet's singing and the soft rushing of the Spring wind. Then the High King turned abruptly and made a sign to Labran, who stepped forward as calmly as he would step to the seat of judgment, and took the brand from Patrick's hand.

So Macha's astonished eyes saw the hand of her father lay the torch against the middle of the hut, where the wet branches joined to the dry. A moment, and the dry wood flared, and the gasp of the people rose with the first spurt of scarlet flame. Then the wind took it, whipping the kindled flame along the roof and into the tangle of wet greenery, fanning it to a strength that could not spurt to flame in the damp wood. Smoke poured in gray, pungent clouds through the side of the hut where Lucran sat, and the flames died on the dry end of the roof. Benet coughed a little and sang on, and the wild gusts of boisterous wind tried again and again to kindle flame, but only succeeded in making more clouds and clouds of suffocating smoke, all carried, as Patrick had foreseen, away from Benet and through the other half of the hut. There was no sound from Lucran; only on the other side, the slightly hoarse, but clear and happy singing of the boy.

Leary watched in silence, immobile, his thumbs stuck in his girdle, and behind him, Lucran's minions stared, cowed and bewildered, and did not move to help him. Labran's face creased a little with pity. He dropped the smoking brand still in his hand, and moved a little closer to the King.

"Leary, my cousin," he said. "Should we not save the Druid? The Roman has made his point."

Leary did not move.

"Let it be as it is," he said. "Let it be as it is. The Druid took the challenge, and did not think beyond that. Now let him make the payment."

Slowly the pouring clouds of smoke were dying away, the green wood too wet even for the wild wind to kindle, and when at last it was the merest whisper spiraling from the shriveled branches, Patrick moved forward and opened the door on the dry side that still stood intact. Benet ceased his singing and came out. He was unharmed and unmarked, his face a little blackened by the gusts of smoke. But the Druid's cloak which lay around his shoulders was burnt in many places, and the smell of scorched wool was sharp and acrid on the clear air.

Patrick took him by the hand and led him toward Leary, and then turned him to the people.

"Here is the hostage I gave to my God," he cried, and the clear beautiful voice rang in triumph and thanksgiving over all the Hill. "My generous God has given him back to me unharmed." He turned to the Druids. "Show the people now," he said, "the hostage which you placed there for your faith."

They huddled together and looked at each other, unwilling to bring into the open the thing that they knew they would find in the other end of the hut.

"You took your challenge," barked Leary in the end. "Show us your proof of power."

They all moved together then, cowed and shamefaced, to drag out the poor suffocated heap of clothing that was Lucran, his smoke-grimed face purple and twisted with the struggles of his death, the silken cope blackened but unharmed around his body. The crowd made no sound; only something like a long, wordless sigh seemed to escape them, and all their eyes rested on Patrick.

Leary turned to him as they dragged away the dead Lucran.

"It is enough, Roman," he cried for all to hear. "It is enough. You are wise and clever, and will not lead my people far astray. They are simple, led to you easily by signs and portents which they do not understand, and now they will listen to your teaching. I am not so simple, Roman! And while I give you my permission and my protection to preach your faith in all my land and kingdom, I bid you at the same time not to trouble me with your God. I will die with the beliefs I have lived with." He turned and looked with strange gentleness at his wife who stood behind him. "You have taken my Queen," he cried. "Now, oh Roman, take my people. But do not trouble me."

Patrick's heart was sick with joy, brimming with gratitude to his unfailing God, the battle over and the victory won. He turned from Leary to the great crowd on the Hill, and never in all the days of his preaching did the happiness of his faith so pour out in his beautiful voice as it did over that multitude on Tara. Words flowed out of him perfect and unsought, as he told them clearly and simply of the God he brought to them, of His life and His death, and His eternal love for every single one of them. He took the things that they had always known in the shape of their beliefs; the colored winds and the Sun; the pale Moon beyond the crystal shell of the sky. He told them how all these things were but the gifts of God.

"God, whom we announce," he said, and his voice was

like a bell that pealed above their heads, "is the ruler of all things; He gives life to all; He upholds all; He gives light to the Sun; He imparts splendor to the Moon. His Son is co-equal and co-eternal with himself. And the Holy Ghost from them proceeds."

He looked at the faces that had drawn close around him, and saw them blank and puzzled, not understanding. Their King spoke truth, he thought. They are a simple people. How can I tell them?

He looked down in thought and almost in despair to the ground under his feet, and saw beside them a patch of the small green, creeping plant which grew all over the moist, cool land of Erin. What better to tell them with than the tiny plant of their own green country? With a cluster of shamrocks in his hand, he lifted up his head again, and bade them see how on the small plant the three leaves were supported on one stalk, and yet were all one leaf. So on the high crest of the sacred Hill of Tara, he saw the light dawning in the puzzled faces, and brought the people to the understanding of the Holy Trinity.

In the end his voice was raw with hours of talking, his face gray with weariness, and the small shamrocks wilted in his hand, but the Christian fire had been kindled now on the Druid Hill itself, and would spread its message to all the land, and he was well content.

His followers made a circle around him and led him away to rest, keeping off the people who would now have crowded to follow him everywhere he might walk. In the moving throng, Macha struggled to come up with him. If she could even reach Benet, he would be able to get her close. But they were all swallowed up by the press of people, determined to follow the priest as far as they might. Only when they realized that they could go no further did they turn away, and the crowds thin out. Macha by then could get no further than the outside of the high door of the Guest House, firmly closed against all comers so that the exhausted Patrick might rest in peace.

She stood and laid her baffled head against the cool, rough wood. Sitting there below him on the Hill, she had felt the same enchantment that had led her from the dun of Sescnen, and her promise to follow his God had come up clear and true in her mind, renewed by listening again to the truths she had come steadfastly to believe. But now, whether she would or not, the greater part of her mind was given over to Kiann with secret pleasure and delight, and she knew that to marry him was the desire of her own heart as well as her father's will. Most desperately she had wanted to see the priest again, to tell him of her muddled mind, and ask him what was right for her to do.

Her father's Steward found her there outside the door, sent to search for her when she was found missing, in company with most of the Household. To her surprise her father did not scold her for running out. He seemed quiet and abstracted, as he often was if he had a great problem of law to solve, and her mother, too, sat and stared into the fire as if she saw there things which she had never seen before. Macha left them in their quietness, and went on into her grianin, her mother lifting her head to tell her half-heartedly to braid her hair and tidy herself, tumbled and disheveled as she was from her fighting through the crowds.

She sat when she was finished at the window of her grianin, and the sound of steps on the ladder of the grianin did not disturb her, or make her lift her tired and troubled head from where she rested it on the wooden frame. She thought it was her bondmaid come to kindle the evening lamps. But the woman made no sound and bore no light and in the end Macha turned.

In the gentle shadows, his head reaching almost to the painted ceiling, Kiann stood within the curtains of her door.

She could find no strength to move. She gaped and

stammered and tried to say all the things she knew to be proper, such as that he should not come here unattended, nor should she entertain him in any case, before their wedding day. All she could manage was to open her mouth in silence, and the sweet weakness that overwhelmed her whenever she saw him was so multiplied by his closeness that she seemed almost to swim away, and watch her dumb self from some painful distance.

"It is well," said Kiann kindly, and smiled at her, and she collected herself enough to notice the great happiness of his face. "I have spoken with your parents, and they said that I might come and talk with you alone."

Still she could not answer.

"May I not sit down, Little Red One," he asked then gently, and at last she mustered her manners, and stood up to make him welcome, offering him the best padded stool to sit on. She sat down opposite him then, her eyes as big as saucers on his face.

Kiann in his turn felt his splendid athlete's body grown suddenly monstrous and unwieldy; too huge to put safely anywhere in this painted women's room; gigantic against the frail looks of the slight girl beside him. Macha saw no ungainly monster. She saw Kiann of the Crimson Cup, with his long fair hair new-brushed and shining like the evening sun, and the last light gleaming in his Champion's Collar and the gold bracelets on his wrists. His cloak was Royal Blue, thick with embroidery over the pleated saffron linen of his fresh tunic. She thought she had never seen him look so splendid. She blinked and wondered if he might vanish like a dream.

He did not vanish. He would have been happier on a battlefield, but this he had to do for Macha's happiness, and he faced it like a warrior, looking down first for courage at his huge skin shoes planted in the rushes.

"Macha," he said, and she started at her name as if she

had never heard it before. "I know that you are troubled about our marriage, since you made a promise to yourself to follow the God of Patrick. This is true?"

He stopped and she nodded dumbly, big tawny eyes still fixed on his face.

"They allowed me for a while to speak with Patrick," he said, "and we talked together of all this." His contentment blazed in his face, and for the first time she saw the love and gentleness in the blue eyes that rested on her, and dropped her own in sudden shyness. "He bids me tell you," Kiann went on, "that you do not have to follow him in person, in order that you may follow his God. I have asked him if I may be baptised a Christian, and you also. We would marry, my Macha, as Christians, so that all our life, he said, would be a following of God, and you have no need of broken vows. This I promise you, is true."

At last she found her voice, hoarse and difficult.

"You have told these things to my parents?"

"I have. They are content. Nor do I think that they will be long in doing the same thing. Your father respects a strong and honest man, and now he will listen to Patrick."

Macha sat a long time in silence, looking out past him to the sky that darkened to purple dusk, thinking over all he had said, and letting the melting happiness pour through her bones. Kiann watched it growing on her face in the last light, and knew that, when he had waited for her all his life, there was no need to hurry her now for her answer.

At last she turned back and looked at him, and the soft freckled face broke into a smile of pure happiness, but the shadows could not hide the light of mischief in the tawny eyes. She lifted a hand and pulled sharply at one of his long, fair curls.

"You used," she said happily, "to get *very* angry when I did that."